The Mile High Cub
Copyright©2016 Jimi Goninan
ISBN 978-1-911478-00-3
Cover art and design by Dawné Dominique

This edition contains both new material and some content previously published as two short stories by Lydian Press.

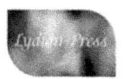

Published by
Lydian Press 2016
Find us on the World Wide Web at
http://www.lydianpress.com

Serviced with a smile!

Time to buckle up it's going to be a bumpy ride…

Flying high with Alex Mathieson, who embraces life as an ever-so-friendly air steward with gay abandon. Until, that is, he falls for a handsome pilot, Peter, and a drastic decision sees him heading into unchartered territory, which may change his life forever.

THE MILE HIGH CUB

Jimi Goninan

Lydian Press

For Peter

A true friend who I sorely miss.

PART ONE

If that little monster doesn't stop screaming I'm going to fold him up and stuff him in the overhead compartment!

Alex Mathieson focused his professional glare on the brat in 14E, as the child continued to treat the entire cabin to a most epic tantrum – all over a missing toy, apparently. He could feel a headache starting to build, so Alex retreated to the galley, and saw his tired, cerulean-blue eyes reflected back at him in the small corner mirror. After smoothing a few errant strays of his chestnut-brown hair back into place, Alex briefly closed his eyes and started to gently massage his temples. His fingers moved in small, deliberate circles, in an effort to release the pain-inducing tension. Not for the first time, Alex questioned his choice of career…as well as the ethics of sedating children for travel.

When he was little, Alex had dreamed of being a pilot but things hadn't quite worked out as planned. Granted, he still got to fly, which he truly loved, however it was far less glamorous than he'd imagined it would be. Not that he disliked his job as a flight attendant, but, as with any position that involves dealing with the public, there were always going to be those with an inflated sense of self-importance who seemed intent on making his life a living hell. On the upside, irritations were fleeting and the perpetrators soon disappeared with their valuables – and equally precious attitudes – at the end of each flight. Thankfully, the majority of the passengers weren't horrible; in fact, some were absolute sweethearts, and seemed to have grasped the fairly rudimentary concept that one doesn't need to be a demanding troll in order to be treated to good customer service.

To be honest, some days it felt like he was little more than a glorified hall monitor-waiter-indentured servant, but there were still quite a lot of perks. Alex was able to visit a multitude of foreign cities while working and was eligible for ridiculously cheap flights during his time off. Not to mention some of the eye candy on display – particularly in the summertime when Pride hit Europe with full force, filling the planes with gorgeous gays off to celebrate in Berlin, Barcelona and the like. Sadly, that was all over for another year, as the Northern Hemisphere had already begun to slip into the increasingly chilly embrace of autumn.

Then there was the matter of the Mile High Club, which Alex had not only joined, but was practically president of – given all the highflying hijinks he'd gotten up to over the past few years. There was nothing quite like the furtive, hurried bouts of passion with friendly strangers, the prospect of being caught by co-workers or passengers only adding to thrill of it all. There were, however, certain crews where it was much easier to get away with it, especially if they were guilty of the exact same transgression. This was hardly limited to the stewards, as some of the stewardesses had been known to put even the sluttiest of gays to shame. Indeed, Alex had come across them giving a helping hand to pilots and passengers more times than he could count, although given the usual high caliber of their conquests he could hardly blame them. For the most part, they all did their very best to keep the skies ever-friendly.

Alex had been with Europe Air for a little over three years. He had completed his two-month training just after his twentieth birthday and had been flying ever since. So far he had only worked for Europe Express, which offered short-haul trips throughout the Continent. Even though they were a low cost airline, they still catered to those who had a bit more money to splash about the place and didn't wish to feel like they were traveling in a cramped, flying bus. To this end, all the planes within their small fleet of Airbus A320s had a small section devoted to business class that offered a free glass of champagne upon boarding and a discreet curtain that kept them separated from the unwashed masses.

Lately, Alex had been thinking about doing the further training necessary to make the switch to long-haul flights with the other branch of the airline – Europe International. The pay was better and it meant that he'd have more time to spend in exotic destinations. Alex also wanted a change of pace but didn't fancy shifting careers completely.

Based in London, Alex adored living in the bustling metropolis but he still relished the chance to spend time in more relaxed locales. This love of travel had also undoubtedly contributed to his interest in vintage postcards. He had started collecting them on the annual trips he taken with his family, when he was a teenager, and over the years it had developed into a keen hobby with Alex often scouring second-hand stores for new additions to his collection.

His schedule kept him quite busy, and this week was no exception, with daily trips to Paris, which meant three flights a day and spending alternate nights there and in London. The airline rented serviced apartments in most of their destinations, as they found it far more cost effective than using hotels and the crews appreciated the extra creature comforts. They had to share rooms but the crews usually got along well enough and sometimes the prospect of sharing a bed with a co-worker wasn't particularly unappealing.

On this schedule Alex was paired with Sam and Ryan, two bubbly blonds he'd worked with on and off since he'd started with the airline. Both were only a few years older than Alex and quite good company. Indeed, they all performed well together – in more ways than one – often joking and helping each other through the most trying of shifts. Sam was the one who had given Alex his nickname of 'Mile High Cub' – due to his hairy, slightly stocky, yet solid, build and willingness to meet any needs his more handsome passengers may have.

They were due to arrive in Paris in about thirty minutes and Alex couldn't wait to land. It was their last shift of the day and he was keen to hand their passengers off onto other service professionals and unwind with his friends.

Damn I need a drink!

* * *

The flight arrived on schedule at Charles de Gaulle, around nine in the evening, and as soon as all the passengers had been cleared from the plane, Alex made his escape. He grabbed his compact, purplish-blue luggage and headed straight to the restrooms to relieve himself, before he had to meet with the others to catch the shuttle to their apartment.

As Alex entered the restroom he almost ran face-first into a middle-aged man in a dark-gray suit that was on his way out.

"Sorry," said Alex automatically.

"No problem," came the husky, deep-voiced reply.

Alex paused in the doorway briefly, watching the man walk away. The gentleman in question had quite a plain-looking face, but what had caught Alex's attention was the large, bodybuilder-like frame straining against the suit. It reminded him of Peter – his favorite fuck-buddy back in London – who had a very similar, rock-solid build. They had been playing together for about five years now and they'd always gotten along really well, personally as well as sexually. Peter was one of the first guys he'd met on the gay scene and it was actually due to Peter's influence that Alex had applied to work for Europe Air – Peter having piloted for them for a number of years. He used to fly the short-haul trips within Europe but had since moved on the longer, trans-continental flights. Sadly, this meant that the pair didn't get to play as often of late due to their conflicting schedules.

At thirty-four, Peter was a fair bit older than Alex but it didn't particularly matter to either of them. Alex had been drawn to the pumped-up pilot from the first time they'd seen each other at a mutual friend's cocktail party – lust at first sight. It had helped that Peter had an imposing, muscular body, with distinguished-looking salt and pepper hair and a devilishly handsome face...the fact that he also happened to be a decent guy was an unexpected bonus.

The pair had been playing with each other for so long that they knew how to get the other revved up in a heartbeat. Not to say that their sex had become formulaic; it just meant they got to each other's pleasure spots far quicker than a stranger. They tended to fuck hard and nasty, with the occasional bout of tenderness thrown in for good measure. Sometimes their games got quite rough, which had left them both with bruises and marks that they tried to cover the best they could, lest friends and co-workers tease them...besides love-bites don't look particularly professional.

Alex much preferred to catch up at Peter's apartment as the pilot lived alone, meaning they could fornicate all over the place and make as much noise as they wanted. Not that they couldn't play at Alex's place. Indeed, Alex's flat mate, George, openly encouraged Alex in his manly pursuits. If truth be told, he was quite the social lad himself, and had a regular procession of gentlemen callers through the apartment – understandable, given he was in his early thirties, built like a lumberjack with a ruggedly handsome face and a package that seemed to bulge indecently no matter what type of pants he wore. Alex often joked that George had been ridden more times than the Tube, which his frisky flat mate never even vaguely attempted to deny. That aside, they both kept their shenanigans contained to their respective bedrooms and tried to be a little respectful of each other when it came to noise levels.

To be honest, Alex had been thinking about Peter more and more lately – and not just how good the pilot's cock felt when it was driving him hard...although that certainly made its way into his masturbatory fantasies on a regular basis. Alex was beginning to wonder if it wasn't perhaps time for him to be a bit more serious about his love life and possibly settle down. He knew that Peter had been interested in pursuing a relationship after they'd been messing around for a few months but it wasn't to be. Unfortunately, at the time, Alex had been new to the pleasures of man-on-man coupling and was only really concerned with fucking as many guys as he could get his hands on – which turned out to be quite a few – so Peter had let the matter drop. Yet, Alex kept coming back to Peter, unwilling to commit but unable to resist.

Brushing his thoughts of Peter to the side, Alex went into the second cubicle from the end. He had just finished his business when he heard somebody enter the cubicle next to his. Alex didn't think much of it, but as he lent forward to start pulling up his black work trousers he noticed that there were two different shoes facing each other, just under the wall of the adjoining stall. His suspicions were soon confirmed when one of the shoes moved back and he could see the jeaned leg of someone going down on their knees. Wanting to satisfy his curiosity, Alex pulled up his pants, without doing up the button fly, and quietly closed the toilet lid. He gingerly stepped up onto the seat of the toilet and had a sneaky peek over the cubicle wall.

The scene below was quite erotic, although Alex was a tad surprised to see that one of the participants was none other than Sam – his comely co-worker – who was being fellated by what looked to be a barely legal, brown-haired lad. Alex was more than a little envious, as he was well aware of how tasty those nine inches of uncut meat were – his mouth began to water at the memory.

The crisp white shirt of Sam's uniform was unbuttoned completely, showing off his slim, bronzed torso and toned abs, with his trousers and underwear pushed down around his ankles. His hands were gripping the back of the young man's head, while he was gently thrusting his sizable cock into the open mouth before him.

Alex took himself in hand and was rather enjoying the unexpected spectacle to which he was being treated. Even so, he was trying to be quiet as possible so as not to be caught by the couple – or anyone else coming into the toilets for that matter. Alex hazarded a guess that this was far from the first headjob that the enthusiastic lad on his knees had given, judging by the way he corkscrewed up and down on the manhood and Sam's appreciative moans.

He certainly seems to know what he's doing. Pity he's not doing it to me.

After a few minutes, Sam pulled the young man to his feet, gave him a passionate kiss before he squatted down in front of him, presumably to return the favor. As he moved downwards he pulled down his playmate's dark-blue distressed denim jeans and then proceeded to bury his face in the lad's crotch. This time Alex was jealous of the stranger, as he knew well the talents Sam's mouth and tongue. Alex was further excited when Sam's companion lifted his baggy white t-shirt over his head to reveal a beautifully defined stomach and solid chest, which had a sprinkling of light-brown hair.

The lad was now making more noise than Sam had, his sighs and gasps increasing in volume as Sam apparently tried his best to bring the boy off to a happy ending. Luckily, the toilets weren't particularly busy at this time of night and no one had come in since they started playing.

Alex was very much enjoying the show as the young man started moving his lean hips faster and faster while Sam worked away on his knees. Only a minute or so later, the boy grabbed Sam's shoulders as his body tensed up, his pleasing features contorting in pleasure. He gave one last thrust before crying out and shooting straight into the flight attendant's mouth. Alex knew that Sam would happily drain the boy dry, as he'd often done the very same thing to him. It was a habit they shared, Alex was a self-confessed cumivore of many years standing. A twinge of hunger swept from Alex's mouth and down to his stomach.

Mmm...I'd love a taste.

Sam then stood up and kissed the young man before turning around and jacking himself over the toilet. It only took thirty seconds of frantic handiwork before he too reached his final release. Sam turned back and embraced the young man again, but this time with a soft, lingering kiss. The two of them then pulled up their pants and rearranged their clothing before having one last quick peck on the lips and exiting the cubicle.

After they had left the restrooms, Alex, who was extremely close to his own release, climbed back down to the floor. He then wanked himself over the toilet as Sam had done – no mess, no fuss. Alex was so worked up it only took a handful of strokes before his semen shot downwards into the water, his body shuddering with every spurt. Once he'd finished unloading Alex quickly wiped himself clean, buttoned up his pants and left the cubicle.

Rushing to the meeting point for their shuttle – he didn't want to keep the others waiting – Alex smiled to himself at the delightful naughtiness of what he'd just witnessed. Fortunately, the shuttle was only just pulling up when he arrived. Alex loaded his luggage in the trunk, climbed on board and took the seat next to Sam. He leant to the side and whispered in Sam's ear.

"I saw what you got up to, you dirty little tramp."

Sam appeared shocked for all a second before he grinned, his bright green eyes practically sparkling with mischief.

"He tasted as good as he looked."

* * *

Despite the heavy traffic, the shuttle ride only took thirty-five minutes and they were soon wheeling their overnight luggage into the apartments – the stewards were sharing one together while the pilots were staying in another just across the hall. Both apartments were sparsely furnished but clean and the beds were big and comfy...the latter a most important consideration for Alex who could be a real bear if he didn't get a good night's sleep.

After changing out of their uniforms into the more comfortable apparel of jeans, t-shirts and light jackets, the trio of stewards decided to have a drink together at a small wine bar down the street but the two pilots pleaded tiredness and stayed behind. The pilots, Rick and Marion, were married to other people but rumor had it that they were fucking on the side, so the boys weren't overly surprised that they'd opted to stay in.

Bet they'll be going over their cockpit maneuvers...dirty sods!

Around midnight, after they'd polished off two bottles of rosé, the bartender started to pack away chairs at the nearby tables. Taking the hint, the boys settled their tab and meandered outside.

"OK, I'm off to have some fun," proclaimed Ryan.

"Gym Louvre?" asked Alex, guessing his friend was headed to the nearby gym-sauna.

"You got it!"

"Have fun, don't do anyone I wouldn't," said Alex with a wide smile.

"So, no limits at all then," added Sam cheekily.

Alex playfully smacked Sam on the arm. They said their goodbyes and Ryan swiftly headed off down the street, clearly anxious to find some friendly foreigners. Left to their own devices, Alex and Sam returned to the apartment. As soon as they were inside the front door Sam pushed Alex up against the wall and kissed him hard.

"So you liked what you saw in the toilets, you little perve?" teased Sam, as they broke for air.

"Damn straight!"

Sam opened his mouth to say something else but Alex silenced him with a hungry kiss. They clumsily made their way to the main bedroom, as they pulled at one another's clothing. Fortunately, Alex had left some lights on so they weren't left stumbling around in the dark as well. By the time they reached the bed they were completely naked, having left a trail of crumpled clothes in their wake. Sam pushed Alex down onto the bed and jumped on top of him. Rolling around kissing and rubbing together, the duo enthusiastically took to the task at hand.

Sam suddenly flipped Alex onto his back and moved down to take Alex's mouth-watering meat down his experienced throat – well, he had been at it since he was barely sixteen. He fondled Alex's hairy balls, holding them firmly as he devoured the eight juicy, uncut inches in his other hand.

To Alex's delight, Sam worked the shaft with his tongue and mouth, increasing the suction as he pulled off the cock slowly. Alex squirmed and grabbed the back of Sam's blond head to bring him in closer, happily enjoying what the young man at the airport had had before him.

After a little while, Alex pulled Sam back up to face level and fervently kissed him again, their sweaty bodies forcefully grinding against each other. Alex wanted to return the favor, so he flipped Sam onto his back before he moved downwards, sucking and biting Sam's erect brown nipples, then licking his underarms and along the smooth stomach before getting to the main prize. Once there, Alex ably gave Sam's crotch a good worshipping as befitted a cock of such beauty. He worked the thick shaft with his mouth, his saliva soon coating every last bit. Alex gently tugged on Sam's large, hairless balls, while his head bobbed up and down on the magnificent manhood before him. He was encouraged in his endeavors by the groans coming from above and the way Sam's hands were strongly grasping at his head and shoulders. Alex could have continued to eat it all night but he had another treat in mind.

Alex knew well from experience that Sam loved having his ass played with – by tongues, stubble, fingers, toys…and best of all, nice big solid cocks. To please his friend – and himself – Alex moved himself further down the bed, grabbed Sam by the hips, lifted him up and exposed the tight hole. Normally, Alex liked to take his time rimming, teasing around the hole before shoving his face deep inside. Tonight, however, the rosé had given him a ravenous appetite and he dived straight in without warning. Alex's tongue pushed and prodded, trying to force its way inside the tight, musky passage.

Sam writhed on the bed, evidently enjoying the invasion. He pressed his hand firmly against the back of Alex's head, which Alex took as a sign to try and open his friend up even further. To gain easier access, Alex lifted Sam up higher so that his hips were resting on Alex's chest and then spread Sam's lean, tanned legs even wider. He stopped rimming and started using his fingers to probe and pleasure the warm, moist tunnel. Sam's moans became louder and louder, echoing throughout the room and encouraging Alex further. Then, in an effort to get his friend even more worked up, Alex alternated between rimming and roughly fingering the pink rosebud.

Unsurprisingly, Sam was leaking precum all over himself; Alex's thick fingers and tongue violating his ass having had the desired effect. After only a few more minutes of such sublime treatment Sam was obviously in need of something more substantial. Happily, for the young steward, Alex had proved time and time again that he knew exactly what to do with his fine piece of meat and how to service an eager bottom correctly.

"Please, I want you in me!" begged Sam.

"My pleasure."

Alex eased Sam back down to the bed before quickly getting up and grabbing condoms and lube from his toiletry bag in the bathroom. He rolled the rubber on as he made his way back to the bed and then coated his manhood in lubricant. Alex reached down with his sticky hand and forcefully fingered Sam once more to make sure he was good and ready to be taken.

Sam gasped as the fingers penetrated roughly inside, but he seemed more than eager for what was to come. When Alex withdrew his hand Sam grabbed it and pulled Alex back down to the bed. Pushing Alex onto his back, Sam then straddled him, positioning the cockhead against his hungry hole. He grunted as Sam sat straight down on his throbbing member, apparently desperate to have it all inside of him – not that Alex minded in the slightest.

Even though he had a firm grip on Sam's hips, Alex was happy to let his cocky co-worker take the lead – for the moment at any rate. He loved the feeling of the tight, velvety passage and very much enjoyed the view as Sam leaned forward and then arched backwards, ensuring that the cock hit all the right angles.

Picking up the pace, Sam rode Alex like a cock-starved cowboy…lifting up and then slamming himself back in the saddle, as his own thick cock bounced up and down, dripping precum all over Alex's hairy stomach. Alex felt the well-trained ass muscles milking his cock, as Sam moaned and groaned, obviously enjoying the stiff rod poking, probing and pleasuring his insides.

Several sweaty minutes later, Alex wanted to take back control, so keeping his tight hold of Sam's hips he flipped them both over, placing Sam on his back. Sam yelped in understandable pleasure as the cock turned inside him. He was clearly happy to be treated in such a rough and tumble manner – sometimes a guy just needs to be fucked like a dirty dog.

And what a naughty little puppy he is.

Alex grabbed a hold of Sam's ankles, stretched out his friend's legs and then started plowing hard, causing Sam to cry out with a look of absolute ecstasy upon his face. The slapping of skin and sounds of satisfaction reverberated throughout the bedroom. Sweat started to drip off of Alex's furry chest and onto the rippling six-pack of the man beneath him. He pounded away without mercy, slamming inside the passage again and again. After a few furious minutes he couldn't hold off any longer and sprayed his hot load into the protective sheath.

Despite his release, Alex kept thrusting so that Sam could get his happy ending too. For his part, Sam was jacking himself frantically and it only took fifteen seconds of stroking before he was spurting his warm, sticky seed all over his tanned torso.

When Sam had unloaded completely, Alex collapsed down on top of him and kissed him gently. Slowly, Alex's cock began to soften and slid out of the warm embrace of Sam's ass of its own accord. Alex cast the condom to the side and resumed kissing and caressing Sam, while their breathing returned to normal. They remained like this for about half an hour before their re-hardened cocks demanded attention. Naturally, they ended up playing again, with Alex topping for a second time, but it was a much slower, more tender affair, as they took their time to reach their sweet release.

Once they were well and truly drained the dirty duo climbed into the shower and washed each other down, rinsing away all the cum and lube before toweling off. Sam jumped straight into bed while Alex made sure that the front door was locked and turned off the lights. Ryan had a key so Alex wasn't worried about his co-worker being able to get back in.

If he ever finishes whoring about Paris.

Then Alex climbed into the bed with Sam and spooned him from behind – he loved going to sleep holding a hot man in his arms…who wouldn't? They were just starting to doze off when they were rudely awoken by the sounds of someone banging around the apartment.

In an apparent effort to not wake up his co-workers, Ryan had entered the apartment in darkness but ended up disturbing them far more than if he'd just turned on the light.

"Come in here, trashy." Alex sleepily called out.

Alex turned on the small bedside lamp to save Ryan from bumping into anything else on his way and his coworker soon found his way inside.

"How was it?" asked Sam.

"Get that itch scratched?" taunted Alex.

"And then some!" Ryan beamed with delight.

He then enthusiastically recounted his adventures, which had ended with him on his knees in the movie room of the sauna and the creamy loads of five random guys raining down on him from above. This didn't particularly surprise either Alex or Sam, as they were used to Ryan regaling them with such sordid stories…and much worse. Ryan's boyish good looks, cheeky smile and ripped body meant that he was quite the popular lad. Truthfully, Alex was a tiny bit jealous of Ryan's exploits. Not that he was lacking for male companionship but sometimes he almost felt like a nun in comparison to his ever-welcoming friend.

"Alright, bedtime for me," declared Ryan, as he turned to head out the door.

"Don't be silly, why don't you just jump in with us?" offered Alex.

"Yeah, there's plenty of room," added Sam, wriggling towards the side of the bed.

Ryan shrugged, then stripped off his clothes and climbed into bed, squeezing in between his friends without any argument. It was hardly the first time they'd been in a bed naked together, after all.

"Mmm, smells like you two had fun," teased Sam.

The sheets still held the faint traces of men at play – a pleasant mix of perspiration and cum.

"That we did." Alex reached up and switched off the lamp, plunging the room back into darkness.

Settling back into the bed, Alex enjoyed the sensation of his friends' warm, naked flesh pressed up against his own. Cozily cuddled up together, the trio drifted off to sleep quickly; the three of them were understandably tired after their manly adventures.

* * *

The irritating high-pitched beep of his alarm penetrated Alex's subconscious and woke him from a most pleasant dream where he was on stage singing a duet with Kylie Minogue, as part of a private concert for the Royal Family. He should have known it was a dream, given that his true singing voice sounded like a cross between a cat in heat and a hyena in its death throes.

Alex wasn't too disappointed, however, with the reality into which he woke up, seeing his morning glory was wedged snugly between Ryan's firm buttocks. He wriggled a bit, enjoying the feeling of Ryan's hard body pressed against his. Then Alex felt a hand slowly running down his side and over his ass. Alex lifted his head and saw that the hand belonged to Sam, who was grinning and looking at him through sleepy eyes. The boys began to caress each other with the slumbering Ryan sandwiched between them.

The slow sensual movements were apparently enough to awaken Ryan, who promptly joined in with their morning greetings, as they writhed together in a mess of happy limbs. Before too long the room was full of moans, grunts and sighs. Knowing their time was short; the threesome began to work frantically – fingers, mouths and tongues sliding everywhere – to bring each other off to a rousing finish. Their efforts were soon rewarded with three manly explosions in quick succession.

Alex lay back on the bed to catch his breath, cuddled by Ryan and Sam on either side. The trio made quite the tasty tableau.

"Now that's how you start the day!" exclaimed Alex.

"I'm certainly not complaining," murmured Sam happily.

"Me neither." Ryan smiled smugly.

The repeat alarm on Alex's phone went off a few minutes later, spurring the threesome into action, as it wouldn't do to be late for their first shift of the day. The lads briskly showered one after the other, otherwise it may have taken them far longer – boys can be so easily distracted. Alex was ready first so he popped down to the little boulangerie, just next door, to grab them some pastries for breakfast.

When he got back to the apartment both Sam and Ryan were already dressed in their work uniforms and ready to go.

They ate their croissants and *pains au chocolat* in the shuttle and made it back to the airport with plenty of time to spare. The rest of the day passed in a blur of safety demonstrations, snack service and dealing with mostly pleasant passengers.

Despite being thoroughly sated from the night before, and again that morning, Alex found himself thinking about Peter again.

Do I want something more?

* * *

The next day Alex had rostered off so he'd planned to meet up with Peter at their regular gym, Boys Club, for a workout. The pair had been gym-buddies for almost as long as they been fuck-buddies, when their schedules allowed, and their strenuous workouts were usually followed by an even more intense session in the privacy of one of their homes.

As is the custom, the men-only gym was full of clinking, banging and grunts, as the like-minded gents strived for perfection in between bouts of ogling, gossip and character assassination.

"Last one, Lex. Come on!" encouraged Peter in his deep baritone, while Alex strained beneath him.

They had been there for an hour and were just finishing up with Peter spotting Alex on the bench press. As was usually the case, Alex found himself a little distracted staring straight up Peter's smooth, solid legs towards the bulging crotch, prominently displayed by his customary tight red gym shorts. The sultry sight – combined with the heady musk of masculine exertion that Peter exuded every workout – had Alex's own crotch swelling in anticipation. Sadly, it was not to be as Peter had other plans for the evening.

With a final burst of energy, Alex pushed the bar into the air where Peter firmly took hold and guided it gently back to the rack.

"Not even time for a bit of sneaky head in the steam room?" asked Alex, only half-joking.

"Afraid not. I'm going home to shower but I promise to give you a good seeing to this weekend…if you're still in need."

"Always!"

"Such a naughty boy. Later, Lex."

Peter was the only one who abbreviated his name in such a manner, a fact Alex very much liked, as it was a telling indication of their closeness. The pilot kissed Alex goodbye on the lips and gave him a friendly pat on the butt before heading on his merry way.

Feeling slightly disappointed, Alex headed upstairs to the change rooms. Even though he knew he'd play with Peter again soon, Alex couldn't help but feel a little churlish at being denied his favorite toy.

Is it just the sex, though?

To help clear his mind, Alex enjoyed a leisurely shower, letting the hot water soothe his overworked muscles while he, not so subtly, checked out the other fine specimens of manhood about the place. The gym was predominately gay, so there was a fair amount of cruising and shenanigans in the locker rooms. Even the odd heterosexual man who went there tended to be fairly open-minded…and not opposed to a friendly helping hand on occasion.

Alex was relatively happy with his progress at the gym over the past few years and had built up quite a solid, muscular frame. His one insecurity was his tummy, which was flat but not as rippling and defined as a good many of the other gym patrons. By now, Alex had come to a grudging acceptance that he didn't have the genetics or willingness to follow a strict enough diet to get chiseled six-pack abs. He figured that it hadn't stopped him bedding any number of hot guys, so he was damn well going to have his cake and eat it too...preferably off of an obliging lad's taut buttocks.

After he was well and truly clean – he had stayed to soap himself up in the open plan showers quite a bit longer than strictly necessary – Alex ambled over to have a sit in the steam room in order to help relax his tight muscles.

Upon opening the door, Alex caught a flurry of movement, as the only two men in the small, slippery room rushed back apart and hastily placed towels in their laps, barely disguising their erections. From the bulges, Alex could plainly see that both men were somewhat well endowed. Through the steam they both looked to be in their late twenties and rather handsome. Alex thought he recognized the one on the left – a fairly well-developed redhead with a wonderfully defined body – from previous gym sessions, but the other – a much leaner blond with a dragon tattoo that ran along the length of his torso on the left side – was new to him.

"Don't mind me guys," reassured Alex, as he took his place on the bench facing both the men.

The steamers then cast aside their towels and resumed their activities. Alex watched their efforts with great interest until the redhead beckoned him closer. Any remaining thoughts of Peter rapidly faded away as Alex eagerly moved forward to join their game, a wide smile plastered on his face.

Guess I'll be getting that post-gym workout, after all.

* * *

As part of his duties, Alex was tasked with helping train the new recruits every six months. The 'newbies' had been through the course the airline offered and completed the theory component, but had yet to accumulate much practical experience.

There was a new batch due to start the following Monday and Alex knew that he would have a few of them along with him on his runs to Berlin that week. When he arrived at work, Alex was introduced to his three new charges – Beth, Roger and Simon. All three seemed lovely and eager but there was only one that he was immediately drawn to – Simon. He had short, shaved darkish-brown hair, light-green eyes and an adorable little dimple when he smiled, which was often. Simon was a bit of a pocket gay, standing a good deal shorter than Alex at only five-foot-seven, but was very easy on the eyes.

I wouldn't mind training him nice and hard!

It turned out that he would be working with Roger on the first few flights, Beth on the ones straight after and Simon towards the end of the week. Alex was pleased to find that both Beth and Roger not only knew their stuff, but also were very easygoing and a delight to work with.

Despite her fresh-faced appearance – brunette curls, wide blue eyes and a waif-like figure – Beth dealt effectively with a difficult passenger on her very first shift. Alex was astounded at her patience and how she resisted the urge to strangle the man, especially after he'd demanded to change seats, berated her for the five-minute delay in boarding and indignation at being asked to switch of his laptop for the takeoff. Just watching the childish behavior, Alex had been tempted to 'accidentally' tip a pot of scalding-hot coffee all over the passenger's precious computer… such a pleasant daydream.

When it came time to work with Simon, Alex was also suitably impressed with his ability and friendly manner. It no doubt helped that Alex could barely take his eyes off of Simon's pert little behind that was wonderfully accentuated by the tight-fitting work pants. They flirted as they worked and there was obviously a spark that needed to be set aflame in another setting – preferably naked.

Sadly, it would have to wait, as Alex's schedule was busy with work for the next week or so and his next day off had been earmarked for Peter. It had been over two weeks since they'd seen each other for anything other than the gym and Alex was keen to play with the passionate pilot. He was still a little unsettled in his feelings towards Peter. It wasn't like he suddenly wanted an epic romance but Alex knew that something had changed, for him at least, and he resolved to talk to Peter about it when they met up.

What's the worst that can happen?

* * *

The following Wednesday afternoon, Alex was resting naked in bed, covered in sweat and a good deal of semen. Lying beside him was an equally sticky, and thoroughly exhausted,

Peter. They'd met up for brunch at their favorite café – Happenstance – in Soho, which had predictably led to bed and to their current state.

"Well that sure hit the spot," said Peter, his face beaming with a satisfied grin.

"Several times," murmured Alex contentedly. He moved onto his side and placed his arm over Peter's smooth, strong chest. "So anything planned for tonight or can we spend it defiling one another?"

"Wish I could but I'm actually going on a date."

Alex felt a sudden pang of annoyance at the interruption of his plans, although his face didn't betray his unexpected fit of emotion.

A date? So much for that talk!

"Oh...anyone I know?" inquired Alex, in as casual as manner as he could muster.

"Nah, just a guy I've seen a few times."

Few times???

"OK, cool. What's his name?"

"Ben...why? Don't tell me you're jealous?"

Bristling slightly at Peter's teasing, Alex felt a touch defensive.

"No, don't be stupid."

Alex laughed in a halfhearted manner. Suddenly he got up from the bed, his face was slightly flushed and he couldn't quite meet Peter's eyes.

"Um...I'm going to jump in the shower and then get out of your hair."

"Nah, it's fine. I've got plenty of time."

"It's OK, I have stuff to do. Besides, at your age you need all the beauty prep you can get!"

Peter stuck his tongue out at Alex.

"Thanks a lot!"

"Any time, big boy."

And with that Alex headed out of the bedroom and down the hallway. Despite his attempts to keep the mood light and jovial, by the time Alex reached the bathroom his heart was overflowing with emotion. He quickly hopped into the shower cubicle, turned on the hot water full-blast and lathered himself up. As he washed away the remnants of their play, Alex tried to calm himself down.

Why the hell am I so upset? It's not like we're a couple. Time to get a grip!

Finishing up as fast as he could, Alex went back to the bedroom to retrieve his clothes, which had been cast haphazardly about the floor during their passionate play. As soon as he was dressed, Alex gave Peter a quick peck goodbye on the lips.

"Hey, you OK?" asked Peter, his face a picture of concern.

"Yeah, all good." Alex brushed off the worry. "I'll give you a call later."

Troubled by his thoughts, Alex practically raced out of the apartment and into the elevator. As he slowly descended towards ground level, Alex silently berated himself for his juvenile behavior.

He's done nothing wrong and I'm acting like an overwrought schoolboy! Besides he probably doesn't like me that way any more. I need to be happy with what I've got!

Once on the street, his thoughts began to quieten down, as he focused on the hustle and bustle of the city, and its inhabitants, swirling around him. To protect against the crisp, autumnal night air, Alex wrapped his red scarf securely around his neck and set off for his apartment at a brisk pace. By the time he'd gotten home again Alex had almost convinced himself that his mental tizzy didn't mean anything at all…almost.

* * *

Towards the end of the next week it was announced that the baggage handlers in Paris would be going on strike – practically the French national past time. In response, Europe Express canceled most of their flights for three days to avoid the hassle. Alex's route was one of the ones to be suspended, meaning that he – along with Sam and Ryan – was going to be stuck in Paris for an extra couple of days.

The boys were discussing what to do over the weekend when Ryan came up with a wonderful suggestion of how to fill their time.

"Why don't we head off to La Demence in Brussels?"

"Count me in!" stated Sam enthusiastically.

"Sounds like a plan," agreed Alex.

Alex had heard stories about this particular party from various friends and acquaintances – including Ryan himself, who was practically a veteran – about the hotness of the guys and how debauched things could get, so he was more than happy to go. Besides, he was overdue for a bit of relief. Not due to lack of opportunity, mind you, but he just hadn't felt like it after his last encounter with Peter. Still troubled over his reaction to Peter's date, try as he might, Alex couldn't shake the feeling of disappointment and jealousy. He knew that the mature thing to do would be talk to Peter about his feelings but that didn't seem likely.

Maybe I just need a good cocking?

Without delay, Alex jumped online to make reservations for the train and somewhere to stay. He found a reasonably priced hotel that was within walking distance of the club where the party was being held – very handy after a big night out. After a brief discussion, the trio decided to only book one room, rightly presuming that they wouldn't be spending much time there and it was hardly like any of the three minded being in such close quarters to one another.

Their train left in a few hours, which meant they'd arrive with plenty of time to freshen up before heading out to the party. Luckily, their airline-provided apartment wasn't far from *Gare du Nord*, so Alex and his companions were able to stroll over with their luggage, enjoying a bit of the Parisian cityscape as they went – although Alex could have done without the occasional waft of stale urine as they walked through the odorous streets.

Really, what is so difficult about the concept of using a toilet?

The lads made their train without any hassle and decided to settle in the bar car for the short journey, as it was far less crowded than the rest of the train…and the boyishly handsome gent serving behind the counter certainly didn't hurt either. Predictably, Ryan flirted with the attendant and ended up getting some complimentary snacks to go with their drinks – as well as the guy's number. The scenery whizzed by and before they knew it they were pulling into the station and walking into the lobby of their hotel shortly afterwards.

Once they checked in, they dumped their bags in the surprisingly luxurious – given the price – room and opted to walk around the city for an hour or so, seeing as it was such a nice, warm day. It was a pleasurable enough promenade but apart from a few impressive buildings and pretty parks there wasn't a lot to hold their interest. They grabbed an early dinner together at a cute Italian restaurant – Taste of Sicily – a few blocks away from their hotel that they'd passed by earlier in the day. It had quite the romantic atmosphere – candlelit and cozy – with the mouthwatering scent of garlicky goodness in the air. The romance may have been wasted on the boys but the food certainly wasn't, although they were mindful of not gorging themselves – it wouldn't do to be bloated on the dance floor, after all.

After they got back from dinner the threesome barely resisted the temptation for a quick bout of fucking, choosing instead the far more sensible option of a quick nap so that they were fully rested for a full night of devilment. Clothes were lazily discarded on the carpeted floor and the trio was soon cuddled up together like three mischievous peas in a pod.

While the others dropped off quite quickly, Alex laid awake, his thoughts dwelling on the all-too-familiar subject of Peter. He didn't feel comfortable confiding in Sam or Ryan as neither of them had ever had a serious boyfriend, or even vaguely expressed a desire for one. Not that Alex was tired of randomly bedding beautiful boys, but he couldn't help but feel that perhaps he was missing out by not becoming emotionally involved with his conquests...in particular, Peter.

What does Ben have that I don't? Have I waited too long? Does he even like me like that anymore?

Eventually, Alex managed to nod off and joined his bedmates in their pre-party slumber.

A few hours later, the lads awoke feeling refreshed and ready to see what the night had in store for them. Each of the trio rushed through their ablutions and were ready rather rapidly, all apparently as keen as one another to get to the club. So, sporting the traditional gay party uniform of tight t-shirts and fitted jeans under their coats, they grabbed their valuables and set off at a brisk pace.

* * *

When they arrived, barely fifteen minutes later, they deposited their excess clothing at the coat check before Ryan gave them a tour of the club, gleefully showing them the different bars, dance floors and – perhaps most importantly – where the naughty spaces were located. The latter were fairly deserted, however, as they had arrived so early and the games wouldn't begin in earnest until much later in the evening. The boys wandered back down to the dance floor on the ground level and proceeded to get happily buzzed on beer. They chatted, danced and mingled with the sociable crowd, as the club slowly filled up with all manner of marvelous men.

A few hours later, Sam was the first to go for another look around upstairs, apparently in the hopes of finding a more active backroom, leaving Alex and Ryan on the dance floor. When Sam rejoined his friends some thirty minutes afterward, Alex couldn't help but notice the satisfied smile on his face.

"I'd head up now if you want some fun!" Sam shouted into Alex's ear over the thumping music.

Alex downed the rest of his beer and immediately headed across the dance floor towards the stairs for the upper level, determined to fuck away his romantic notions concerning Peter. He found the first room again easily enough but didn't see anything that took his fancy – not that he could really see all that clearly in the dimly-lit space – so he went back down the staircase and wandered around through a little bar, to the other space. Alex did pause briefly along the way to watch a generously proportioned gogo dancer, who was on the counter of the bar, in an extremely aroused state, much to the delight of the assembled crowd. After filing away some mental images for later use, Alex continued on in his pursuit of pleasure.

The space was even darker than the other backroom had been, but he could hear the agreeable sounds of men pleasuring each other all around him. His nostrils were filled with the unmistakable scent of masculine passion and his crotch swelled in response. Alex knew from Ryan's earlier tour that the space was a series of three rooms, which formed a circle, so he rested against the wall by the entrance for a few minutes to let his eyes adjust to the darkness before he made the circuit. The heat was almost stifling and caused him to take off his vibrant-red t-shirt and tuck it into the waistband of his jeans.

When he could see better, Alex moved further into the room, sliding up against the various moist bodies as he checked out the action and scanned the crowd for potential playmates. He had been watching a muscle bear demolishing the pert ass of a very vocally appreciative twink when he turned around, intending to move into the next room, and ran smack bang into a hard wall of muscle.

"I'm sor…"

Alex's apology was abruptly cut off when the muscleman moved forward and forcefully kissed him on the mouth. Naturally, Alex responded in kind and they were soon grinding up against one another. When they broke for air Alex could see that while the man wasn't classically beautiful he did have a certain rugged appeal. The stranger took him by the hand and dragged him up against the nearby wall where they resumed hungrily kissing.

The stranger reached down and undid Alex's fly, then his own, releasing their erections from their underwear. Grabbing them both in his rough hand, the muscleman massaged the two members together, the wetness of their collective precum coating their cockheads and shafts.

All of a sudden, the stranger yanked Alex's jeans down around his ankles, spun him around and pushed him up against the wall. Then the muscleman ravenously kissed the back of Alex's neck and shoulders before making his way downwards – licking and kissing all the way. When he reached Alex's furry cheeks he spread them wide, his nails digging into the plump flesh, and shoved his face inside.

Alex moaned and squirmed as the tongue expertly explored the tight entrance and did its best to open him up. He pushed back to ride that manly face, enjoying the feel of the stubble as it scratched across his sensitive, hairy hole.

The rimming lasted a few glorious minutes before the muscleman stood back up and grabbed a condom from his pocket. Alex looked over his shoulder and saw the man rolling it down the length his enormous erection – nine extra-thick inches of uncut goodness – and felt his own cock become even harder in anticipation. He turned back to face the grimy wall and soon felt rough fingers pushing their way inside, lubricating his hole and preparing for imminent invasion.

The stranger placed his bulbous cockhead at the moist entrance and shoved it in, biting Alex on the back of the neck at same time, causing the cock-full cub to feel waves of pleasure and pain surging up and down his body. Once the muscleman was firmly within, balls-deep, he rested there, which gave Alex time to adjust to wide inches inside of him. The respite was only temporary and soon the stranger slowly started to move back and forth before pounding away in earnest. He fucked Alex hard, using his powerfully built frame to pin the increasingly sweaty steward against the wall.

Alex panted and moaned as the massive meat mercilessly assaulted his ass. He hadn't had such a brutal hammering – or such a thick manhood – in quite some time and he savored every thrust. The beers he'd drunk had made Alex a bit tipsy, which had the added benefit of relaxing him and helped numb any discomfort from the relentless battering. Even so, he knew that he couldn't take too much more punishment but was reluctant to tell the muscleman to stop.

Fortunately, the stranger appeared to take pity on Alex's poor abused behind and pulled out after only a few more minutes of tough thumping. He ripped off his condom and spun

Alex back around to face him. Once more the muscleman gripped both members in his strong right hand and jacked them together at a frantic pace.

Alex's heart pounded inside his chest, geared up by the excitement of the encounter and his imminent ejaculation. Seconds later, Alex erupted, coating both their dicks in his thick cream. He was followed almost immediately afterwards by the stranger, who'd obviously been just as close to the edge. They resumed kissing as the cum dripped down over their empty balls and thick thighs. A beautiful twink of a boy, who'd been standing next to them, undoubtedly watching their coupling with envy, suddenly sank to his knees and started to lap up their spilt seed.

Neither Alex nor the stranger objected and just continued to kiss as the newcomer cleaned their not-so-private parts completely. Once he was done the lad simply hopped up and disappeared off into to the darkness, presumably to find some other men to similarly service.

The stranger gave Alex one last passionate kiss before he buckled up his pants, gave Alex a sly wink and wandered away. Alex grabbed some paper towels from the nearby dispenser to wipe himself down and pulled up his jeans before heading back to the small bar to grab a drink. The gogo dancer was gone; much to Alex's disappointment, but it meant there were less people and easier access to the bar. He got another beer for himself and a round for his friends.

When Alex rejoined his small group, in the far left corner of the main dance floor, he didn't need to say a thing. His impish grin told them all they needed to know about how well he'd fared upstairs.

It was then that Alex noticed that fortune had seemingly smiled on all three of them that evening. In his absence, it appeared that Ryan had found a new friend in the form of an ebony god of a man with bulging muscles, chiseled features and a dazzling white smile. Indeed, the twosome was practically glued to one another, as they moved together on the dance floor.

"This is William," said Ryan, introducing his comely companion, when they took a small break from molesting one another.

Despite his recent satisfying encounter, Alex found himself a little envious…especially when he saw the outline of an erection that seemed to go most of the way down William's thigh.

Damn that'd feel amazing. Stop being so greedy! Why? It's not like I'm saving myself for anyone.

Roughly an hour later, it came as no surprise to Alex – or anyone who'd been watching the pair dry humping for the past hour – when Ryan announced he was leaving with William to get better acquainted away from prying eyes.

"Is it OK if we use the hotel room? William's friends are already sleeping back at his hotel," asked Ryan tentatively.

"Fine by me, I'll be here for a good while longer," declared Alex.

"Sure, have fun!" Sam smiled amiably.

Alex watched Ryan and William beat a hasty exit, obviously anxious to be naked as soon as possible.

The rest of Alex and Sam's evening was a marvelous mix of dancing, drinking and the occasional kiss with a random stranger. All too soon the music was switched off and the partygoers were forced outside into the cold by the unforgiving glare of the fluorescent house lights. Alex and Sam then joined all the other amused gays as they poured into the street and loitered about. They stood around chatting with some of their fellow inebriated, and extremely sociable, revelers for about ten minutes or so before agreeing to head on their merry way back to the hotel.

* * *

Due to their drunken state, the walk back took the two friends double the time it had to get there – several wrong turns undoubtedly contributed to their delay. When they finally arrived back to the door of their room, Alex was surprised not to hear the sounds of frantic fucking. Upon entering, however, they were treated to the delicious sight of Ryan and William lazily rolling around kissing and caressing one another…and completely oblivious to their arrival.

"Still having fun then?" asked Alex cheekily.

The twosome on the bed ignored them, evidently far more engrossed in each other than anything else.

"Shower?" Sam suggested to Alex.

Given his less than fresh state, Alex readily agreed and the pair went to the bathroom, leaving the boys on the bed to their fun. They stripped off and the refreshing hot water soon rinsed away the sweat and other pleasurable excretions from their tired bodies. Unknowingly, the friends then repeated what Ryan and William had done a few hours beforehand, soaping each other up and gently kissing, while the shower enveloped them in a warm cocoon of steam and water.

They had been in there for about ten minutes when the frosted glass shower door slid open.

"Room for two more?" demanded Ryan, his habitual mischievous smirk firmly in place.

"Always!" Alex excitedly grabbed a hold of their hands and drew them into the shower.

His enthusiastic reaction was completely understandable given the full erect eleven inches William had on display.

I'm surprised he has enough blood to lift it!

It was a tight fit but none of the foursome seemed to mind. The newcomers soon joined in the soapy shenanigans, with hands going everywhere and a lot of thorough cleaning being done. Given the limited space available there wasn't room for anything other than a cozy, old-fashioned circle jerk. Their free hands tweaking, rubbing and generally groping each other, as their bodies pressed together.

All four were so worked up that it didn't take long before load after load was spurting and splashing together on the sea-green tiled floor and each other's feet. Ryan hopped out first, followed by William and Sam. Alex stayed behind to make sure that all the white remnants were washed away, as he didn't want to leave any nasty surprises for the cleaning staff.

It's only polite, after all.

The quartet dried themselves off and trooped back off to the bedroom. The bed proved rather snug with all four men together but they managed to arrange themselves into a contented tangle of bodies. One by one, they drifted off until the room was silent but for the heavy breathing of slumbering men.

Much later that day, when they finally awoke, the frisky foursome began to play anew. After a few hours they had to stop their naughtiness, lest their bits fall off from overuse, and because William had to leave in order to make it back to his own hotel and catch a late train back home. Fortuitously, he lived in London so he swapped details with the lads so they could catch up in their home city.

While Alex would have loved to ride William's amazing appendage again he thought it unlikely to happen. Throughout their playtime he'd seen the looks that were passing between Ryan and William and could plainly see that there seemed to be more going on than just a casual hook-up…surprising given Ryan's predilection for promiscuity, but still.

Of course, thinking along these lines sent Alex's brain right back to the problem he'd been trying so hard to forget.

What do I do about Peter? Have I left things too long? Do I really want a relationship?

* * *

The rest of their stay in Brussels was far less eventful and the trio caught the train back to Paris the following afternoon. Following the end of the strike the flights were completely jam-packed and full of customers complaining about the delay…and just about everything else. Alex took it in his stride and somehow managed to overcome his urge to gag some of the more vocal passengers with their seatbelts – although this became harder and harder as the day wore on.

Finally, the stewards were done for the day and shared a cab back to Soho, as all three lived not far from the gay hub. They said their goodbyes, in a flurry of kisses and hugs, at the end of Old Compton Street and each headed to their respective abodes.

Fifteen minutes later, Alex was walking through his front door, glad to be home after a draining day. He could hear muffled noises coming from George's bedroom down the hallway and correctly assumed that his flat mate was entertaining a visitor. Feeling utterly exhausted, Alex dropped his luggage in his room and collapsed on the bed, quite content to go to sleep in his uniform. It was then that he heard the familiar chime of a received message. Alex wearily raised his head and reached for his phone that he'd left sitting on top of the bedside drawers.

As soon as he saw who the sender was, Alex immediately perked up.

Peter!

Given the late hour it could only be for one thing. He opened the text and sure enough there was a photo of Peter's manhood in all its glory with the words 'all aboard?' in the message.

He was immediately conflicted, as the head located in his crotch wanted to rush right over to Peter's apartment and fuck the night away, while the head above his shoulders thought it was a terrible idea.

I need to talk to him. But the sex will be awesome. Is he still seeing Ben? I don't want to get all possessive and jealous. Stop being a little bitch!

Eventually, his higher head, and tiredness, won out and he discarded his uniform, crawled into bed and switched out the light, all without responding to the text. As sleep overtook his conscious mind Alex still felt a little lost and his heart seemed far too heavy.

Is this what love feels like?

* * *

The following morning, Alex shuffled sleepily into the kitchen in search of caffeine when he came upon the unexpected sight of a muscular, redheaded man, not wearing a stitch of clothing and apparently in the process of making tea.

Am I dreaming?

The naked stranger turned around to reveal startling blue eyes, a friendly smile and a rather plump appendage swinging between his legs.

"Hi, I'm Gus. You must be Alex. Nice to meet you," said the stranger offering his hand to shake.

Alex reciprocated automatically but was even more confused as to what exactly what was going on.

"Would you like a cup of tea?" offered Gus.

"Um…sure that would be nice. Milk with one."

Just then George walked in a similar state of nakedness.

"Oh hi! Sorry, I didn't expect you back till later. I see you've met Gus."

"Yeah, he's making me some tea."

The situation felt all a bit surreal to Alex, although he wasn't particularly opposed to having two nude buff men in his kitchen. Besides, he and George had already spent a few clothing-free weekends when Alex had first moved in. They had both decided to dispense with all that pesky sexual tension straight away, even if their relationship was far more brotherly in nature these days.

"Here you go," said Gus, handing Alex a hot cup of tea. "See you later."

He then grabbed the other two cups and padded off down the hallway to George's bedroom.

"Isn't he gorgeous? We met at XXL on Saturday night and we've been going at it ever since. Can't get enough of each other!" exclaimed George, his enjoyment evident.

"Lucky you." Alex's tone held a trace of wistfulness.

"Did you have a good weekend?"

"Yeah, La Demence was fun!"

"I bet. I haven't been there in years but I lost count of the guys I went through."

George let out a big throaty laugh. Then, apparently noticing a change in his flat mate's normally cheerful demeanor, he switched to big brother mode and put his hand on Alex's shoulder.

"You alright? You seem a bit down."

"Yeah I'm just tired, the flights back were a bit of a nightmare," explained Alex, his manner not particularly convincing.

"You sure?"

Alex nodded a little too enthusiastically.

"Well I'm here if you need to talk," proffered George, clearly not believing Alex's excuse.

"Thanks, I'll be fine."

Am I really that transparent?

"OK. See you in a bit. There's something I need to take care of."

A mischievous twinkle shone in George's warm brown eyes. He affectionately ruffled Alex's messy bed-hair and headed off to join Gus.

Alex took his tea back to his room and climbed back into bed. The sight of all that tempting male flesh made him half-regret not seeing Peter the previous evening.

This is ridiculous. Time to man up!

Before he had time to talk himself out of it Alex picked up his phone and called Peter.

"Hey, handsome," greeted Peter, answering on the third ring. "Missed you last night."

Alex's heart fluttered a little but then he immediately scolded himself.

He probably just means my ass.

"Yeah, sorry. I was super tired."

"That's OK, there's always next time."

"About that. You free today? I kinda wanted to talk to you about something."

"Actually, not really. I'm off to the airport this afternoon."

"When you're back then?"

"Sure, but that's not for three weeks."

Alex sat up dead straight, suddenly panicked.

"What?"

"I'm off to Australia on holidays. Sunshine and beaches here I come!" Peter paused slightly. "Don't you remember?"

"Ah...yeah, that's right. Sorry, I'm still a bit sleepy."

In all his emotional turmoil Alex had completely forgotten about Peter's trip, rather ironic given how obsessive he'd been about the pilot of late.

"What did you want to talk about?" There was a note of concern in Peter's deep voice. "I can make time for a coffee if you need me."

"No...no, it's nothing important. Have a great trip and I'll see you when you're back."

Big girl's blouse! What am I scared of? I'll do it later.

"Look forward to it. Pity about last night but I'll make up for it. Your behind won't know what hit it!" promised Peter laughing.

"Can't wait."

"Bye, beautiful."

"Safe travel."

Alex hung up the phone, lay back in the bed and pulled the covers up over his head.

What is wrong with me?!?

* * *

Two weeks later, Alex was still moping about like a lovesick teenager. It didn't help matters that Gus had practically moved in after that first weekend and now he and George were acting like newlyweds...certainly a change from George's previous revolving door policy. Not that Alex objected to hearing their muffled fucking through the wall or even seeing Gus bare-ass naked in the kitchen most mornings – honestly the boy had no shame – but it did remind him of what was missing from his own life.

The thoroughly cold weather and unrelenting gray, wintry skies were doing nothing to improve his mood. Finding himself at a loose end, Alex debated whether or not he should visit a sauna to get some temporary satisfaction. The decision was made for him when he received a text from his former trainee Simon, inviting him over for a drink. The two hadn't worked together much since Simon's training but they'd kept in touch, exchanging flirty messages on a regular basis. Alex had a sneaking suspicion that a 'drink' would undoubtedly lead to something else but he was in need of the distraction and he guessed that Simon would be an eager playmate.

Alex knew Simon still lived with his parents – he was only eighteen, after all – but that they were away on holidays so they'd have the place to themselves. After getting the address from Simon, Alex jumped in a cab and made his way to Marble Arch. Alex gathered by the size of the house that Simon's family wasn't particularly lacking financially.

He rang the doorbell and was soon greeted by Simon, wearing a tight white polo and even tighter jeans.

"Glad you could come over." Simon gave Alex a chaste kiss on the lips. "Come in."

Alex followed after Simon, as he led him through the house and into the lounge room, which had grand mahogany bookshelves lining the walls. The family was apparently very well-read in addition to being very well-off. Alex adored the distinctive old book smell that seemed to permeate the room, as it reminded him of afternoons spent in his grandparents' small bookshop whenever he'd spent holidays with them as a child.

As Alex examined the bookshelves, noting more than a few valuable first editions, Simon went behind the small, fully stocked bar in the corner.

"Cocktail?" suggested Simon.

"Sure."

Alex was never one to turn down free alcohol. A few minutes later, Simon had produced one of the strongest Orgasms

43

that Alex had ever tasted…and he'd tasted a lot. They then retired to the caramel-brown chesterfield couch in front of the unlit marble fireplace, to drink and chat.

The conversation flowed freely and Alex found that he was feeling better than he had since Peter had left, no doubt helped by the excessive amount of alcohol flowing through his system. The first drink seemed to practically evaporate, a second and third soon followed. Alex had just drained his glass and was well on his way to being sloppily drunk when Simon suddenly pounced. Before Alex knew what was happening Simon was laying on top of him, kissing him with a fierce intensity. Not wanting to be an impolite guest, Alex responded in the only civil way possible and kissed him back.

Their shirts were soon lying crumpled on the floor.

"Mmm…furry," said Simon appreciatively, as he ran his hands through Alex's silky-smooth, curly chest hair.

"Glad you approve."

"Very much so."

Simon moved downwards and took Alex's erect brown nipples in his mouth, one after the other, sucking and teasing them with his teeth. He bit down a little too hard causing Alex to cry out.

"Hey, careful!"

"Sorry," apologized Simon, not looking the least bit remorseful.

Alex laid back into the couch as Simon kissed and licked his way down the exposed, hirsute tummy. Moments later, Simon was unbuckling Alex's belt and button fly, apparently anxious to get to the tasty treat contained within. Simon's nimble fingers soon had the straining erection released and he downed Alex's cock in one big gulp. Alex threw his head back in pleasure as he felt the talented tongue swirling around his member.

Simon kept his face buried in Alex's untamed crotch, obviously enjoying the feel of the bushy brown hair brushing up against his face and the mouthful of manhood. He cupped Alex's heavy balls in his left hand, while his right snaked its way underneath and towards the hairy entrance.

Alex moaned as Simon expertly worked his shaft and balls. He could feel his playmate's slender fingers poking at his hole, eager to be inside. Simon brought his hand back briefly, and put it in Alex's mouth to coat it in saliva before returning it to its position between the plump ass cheeks. He pushed at the hole again and this time his fingers slid in smoothly, the sweat and spit successfully having eased the way. The sensation of the digits exploring his passage, sent jolts of pleasure all through Alex's groin, causing him to gasp his enjoyment.

After a few more minutes of this delightful play, Simon stood up, pulling Alex to his feet and silently led him upstairs to bedroom. Alex was slightly taken aback by how forward Simon was being, given his age, but he was more than happy to enjoy the ride.

Once the door was shut behind them, Simon dragged Alex to the bed, where they thrashed around; kissing and helping strip one another's remaining clothing. They were both naked in a matter of minutes, their hands and fingers exploring each other…grasping, groping and clawing.

Despite noticing Simon's ample package earlier, Alex was still surprised – and thrilled – by the size of his appendage, which almost looked like another limb in comparison to his smaller frame. Alex wasn't a size-queen per se – well, no more than any other gay man – but he still appreciated the beauty of a generous endowment...in this case nearly ten inches of delicious manhood.

I hope he knows what he's doing with that thing!

Showing a strength incongruous with his slight build, Simon effortlessly flipped Alex onto his stomach, roughly separated his solid, hairy legs and shoved his face right in between the round globes of Alex's ass. His long tongue darted inside the tight opening and tasted the tangy passage.

Trying to open himself further to the masterful mouth pleasuring him, Alex arched his back and tilted his hips upwards. He then felt Simon pushing his face in even deeper. Although Alex had made the clichéd assumption that Simon would be a little bottom boy because of his smaller stature, he wasn't complaining about Simon's obvious interest in violating his ass. Indeed, after about ten minutes of that talented tongue teasing his hole, Alex was desperate to be pounded hard and fast...not to say he wouldn't be amenable if Simon wanted to flip-flop later in the evening.

As if he'd read Alex's mind – although anyone who'd heard the moaning would be in no doubt as to what was required – Simon pulled his face away from his lusty work and grabbed the necessary supplies. Lining up his sheathed weapon with the lubricated target, Simon pushed Alex's head firmly into the pillow and shoved his many inches into the pleasant passage.

"Fucking hell!" Alex yelled through the pillow.

Without giving Alex any reprieve, Simon slammed his cock home, again and again. Beneath him, Alex squirmed and struggled all the while cursing Simon profusely, although it was more for show. Once the initial pain and discomfort had faded, Alex was in seventh heaven as Simon took total command of his aching ass.

They energetically rolled around and fucked on and off for a few hours, switching positions so that Simon could attack Alex's well-used hole from every angle. He plowed him over the edge of the bed, on his back, twisted on his side, on his hands and knees…

When he could think straight, between rounds of vicious thrusting, Alex was mightily impressed. He'd been with guys more than double Simon's age that didn't have half his technique and ability to please a man properly. Alex knew he'd been feeling this fuck for some days to come and was glad of it.

Finally, as satisfying as the pounding was, Alex realized that there were limits to his bottoming endurance and grudgingly admitted defeat.

"Please, I can't take any more. I need to cum!" growled Alex.

Simon nodded his agreement and flipped Alex over onto his back so that he could wank himself while continuing to be furiously fucked. He spread Alex's legs as wide as possible and gripped them tightly as he skillfully wielded his weapon.

It took less than a minute before Alex was spraying his well-earned release all over his solid, hairy chest. His ass contracted tightly around Simon's manhood with every spurt of cum, causing Simon to gasp. He was apparently rather close to his own release as well.

Simon hurriedly pulled out, ripped off the condom and shuddered as he ejaculated all over Alex's cock, balls and furry stomach, his happy cries of release ringing through the room. With his orgasm spent, Simon ran his hands through the sticky mess, swirling the two loads together. He then proceeded to slowly lick his hands clean of cum, which Alex found to be an incredibly erotic display.

"We taste great together," declared Simon smugly.

In an apparent effort to prove his point, Simon leaned forward and gave Alex a long, lingering kiss. Alex had to admit he was right; the salty-sweet mix of their seed was delicious.

"We certainly do," agreed Alex, pulling Simon in for a close embrace.

The pair recommenced kissing, their sweaty, manly forms lazily rubbing together. The Orgasms that Alex had drunk earlier, and the amazing one he'd just had all over himself, left him feeling like he could easily glide away. The boys kept smooching, lying together in their post-coital glow, as the perspiration and leftover semen dried on their exhausted bodies – neither of them in a particular hurry to leave.

"Time to wash up?" proposed Simon.

"Lead the way."

The pair then traipsed down the hallway to the nearby bathroom to rinse off. Once in the shower they soaped each other up and predictably became erect again after a few minutes. This time Alex took control and leisurely jacked their cocks together as they kissed. The hot water splashed down over them, helping to soothe their overworked muscles, as Alex kept a firm grip on their members.

When Alex could feel the warmth start to leave the water, he moved his hand faster, in order to bring them both off before they were hit with an icy blast. Alex's efforts were soon rewarded, as Simon's breathing became labored and his body tensed up in orgasm before exploding over the two of them. The sight of Simon's seed coating their crotches pushed Alex over the edge and he too spurted away. A copious amount of cum ran down the shafts and oozed down their wet bodies.

The duo quickly washed up and hopped out to dry themselves on the large, red towels that Simon had grabbed from the linen press on the way to the bathroom. When they were finished they walked out of the bathroom wrapped only in towels and ran straight into a middle-aged couple carrying suitcases – Simon's parents.

"What are you guys doing back?" demanded a clearly exasperated Simon.

"There was a bad bout of food poisoning, so we left the ship at the last port and decided to fly home," explained Simon's father.

"Anyway, it's good to see you dear. Aren't you going to introduce your friend?" inquired Simon's mother in a perfectly polite fashion.

Alex froze, he didn't know how he expected Simon's parents to react to catching their son in such a compromising situation but it certainly wasn't like this. He was more than a little stunned at how unaffected they seemed in this potentially awkward state of affairs. In fact, they were acting like he'd just turned up fully dressed to sit down for a nice Sunday dinner.

"Parents this is Alex, Alex this is Margaret and Phillip," muttered Simon, obviously embarrassed.

"Pleased to meet you," said Alex, with as much dignity as he could muster standing there clad in just a towel.

"And you too, son," replied Phillip.

"Now, don't let us keep you. I'm sure you have plans." Margaret had a knowing smile on her lips.

The pair almost ran down the hallway in their hurry to get back to the security of Simon's bedroom.

"Sorry about that. They are ridiculously open and supportive. Don't worry you're far from the first guy I've had to stay. They've let boyfriends sleep over since I was sixteen."

"That doesn't sound so bad," commented Alex, feeling envious of such a close parental relationship.

"Yes and no. It also means that they feel like they can be just as easy and free with their sex lives. Some sounds children should never hear coming from their parents' bedroom." Simon laughed but there was a strong undercurrent of truth to his words.

"I see your point. Well, I should get going."

"You can crash here if you want." Simon's offer seemed to have a touch of need about it. "I promise my parents will leave us alone."

"Tempting...but I have an early start tomorrow."

It was a lie but Alex felt like being alone. As pleasant company as Simon was, not to mention the amazing sex, the thought of Peter was never far away.

"OK, I'll give you a ride home though. It's late and it's the least I can do after all the riding you let me do." Simon smirked.

"Well, if you insist."

Truthfully, Alex was glad of the offer and made sure to give Simon an extra-long kiss goodbye when they arrived at their destination. He watched Simon drive off and then headed inside his apartment building, sore but sated.

* * *

Ten minutes later, Alex was wrapped up in bed and reflecting on the evening's events. Fortunately, George and Gus appeared to have retired for the evening, with no sounds of sodomy to be heard, so he could think without distraction.

As awkward as encountering Simon's parents had been for Alex, he was still a little jealous. His relationship with his own family was almost the exact opposite. Alex's parents had reacted badly when he'd come out four years previously. They were of the strict Roman Catholic mold and even attended mass every Sunday, come rain, come shine; a growing rarity in today's age. They hadn't disowned him, but he was glad that he'd already moved out of home by then. It had been quite strained between them for well over a year, at which point they'd come to begrudging acceptance of their son's 'lifestyle choice'.

Whatever happened to unconditional love?

Even so, he still had it better than other friends of his who had had absolutely no contact at all with their families since being honest and throwing open the closet door. Although, in cases like that, Alex was firmly of the opinion that if your family was going to be so hateful and toxic then it was better to be far away from them and be with people who actually loved, rather than despised, you for who you were.

Alex had been fortunate in having a good circle of friends that had stuck by him after he'd come out. His older brother and sister, Josh and Ella, had also come to his aid. They were far less religious, and a good deal more tolerant, than they'd been brought up to be. All in all, it hadn't been too traumatic, but it would still be a long time before he'd even think about bringing a guy home to meet his parents. Not that he had any contenders for that position at the moment, unless...

He's dating someone else. Maybe I still have a chance? Stop obsessing, it's pathetic!

And with that self-scolding Alex switched off the light and eventually fell into a fitful sleep.

* * *

Several days after his encounter with Simon, Alex was walking through the busy side streets of Soho, on his way to Happenstance, to grab a Chai Latté. The city was awash with Christmas decorations and there was a feeling of festive goodwill in the air. It was an unseasonably bright and sunny day – rare for London – and Alex was in a particularly good mood. This was indisputably due to the fact that Peter was back in town and they had made plans to meet up that night. Alex was determined that he was finally going to use his balls for something other than decorating the chins of strangers and tell Peter how he felt.

He had just gotten his order to go and turned around to see Peter walking into the café, chatting and laughing with a blond hunk who looked like he belonged on the cover of a Mills & Boon novel – bulging biceps, chiseled jaw, piercing green eyes and perfect floppy hair. Alex stopped dead in his tracks, his happiness evaporated and he felt a sinking sensation in his stomach.

I have no chance.

"Hey, Lex."

Alex managed a weak smile in return and gripped his piping-hot beverage tighter in his hand.

"I'd like you to meet my cousin, Derek. He's just moved to the city. Derek this is Alex."

Oh, thank the gods!

Suddenly, Alex became incredibly sociable, a wide grin lighting up his face.

"So lovely to meet you," Alex said warmly.

"You too. Always good to meet one of PP's friends."

"PP?" queried Alex.

"An embarrassing nickname from childhood," explained Peter looking slightly mortified. "Why don't you grab us some coffees, Derek? Before I tell him about your adventures with the chicken coop and the randy rooster."

"OK, truce!"

Derek put his hands up good-naturedly and wandered over to the counter.

"How was the trip?" asked Alex.

"Fantastic! I'll show you all the pics tonight…well, after we get some other important catching up done first."

There was no mistaking the seductive tone in his voice.

"How's Ben?"

"Who?"

Peter's face was completely blank. Alex began to wonder if he'd misheard Peter and gotten the name wrong.

"Ben…the guy you were seeing?"

"Oh, him. No idea. That fizzled out ages ago."

Alex felt like bursting with joy but managed to keep himself together. Just then Derek came back with fragrant coffees in hand.

"You want to get a table or keep on the move?" Peter asked his cousin.

"Here's good. Why don't you join us? I promise I won't tell too many stories about PP."

Peter shot him a warning look, full of malicious intent.

"Or any at all."

"Nah, I've got to get some errands done," said Alex. "Next time."

"Well I'll see you tonight then," murmured Peter, as he gave Alex a strong peck on the lips, with just a hint of tongue.

Alex said his goodbyes and floated out of the café, buoyed by the kiss that seemed to linger on his mouth. Once in the street he zoomed over to the menswear store across the street to buy the sexiest pair of underwear he could find.

Tonight's the night!

* * *

Alex spent the rest of the afternoon primping and preening, with a huge smile upon his face. After completing his numerous beauty treatments, Alex slipped on his brand-new underwear – a pair of red and black bottomless jocks that cradled his crotch perfectly while exposing his plump posterior to its best effect. He looked at himself in the mirror and was pleased with what he saw.

"Yum!" proclaimed George through the open door. "Big date?"

"Yup, with Peter."

"So, are you going to tell him?"

George had heard all about Alex's complicated emotions on the subject and been nothing but encouraging.

"I think so."

"Good! He'd be crazy not to want to date you properly…especially in that outfit."

"Thanks."

Alex moved over to the door and gave George an affection kiss on the cheek. Just then Gus walked by, naked as usual, on his way to the kitchen.

"Is this a private party or can anyone join in?" the redhead joked.

While Alex certainly wouldn't have minded being tag teamed by his flat mate and Gus, tonight he only had eyes – and every other body part – for one man. Alex gave Gus a peck on the cheek as well so he wouldn't feel left out.

"Maybe another time." Alex turned and shook his butt suggestively at them as he walked over to his wardrobe to continue getting ready.

"We'll leave you to it then," said George, grabbing Gus by the hand.

A few minutes later, Alex heard the familiar sounds of men at play through the adjoining bedroom wall. He just smiled to himself and focused on looking his very best for the night ahead.

After copious outfit changes, which left his bedroom floor looking like his wardrobe had very recently exploded, Alex was finally ready. He grabbed his overnight backpack and walked the twenty minutes over to Peter's apartment building, located in a large complex on the Oxford Street side of Soho. It was on the eleventh level, with floor to ceiling glass walls, which afforded a wonderful view out over the London cityscape. When they'd played of a weekday, Peter was always careful to draw the curtains, as the windows of the office building next door looked right in and gave no privacy whatsoever. Of a nighttime, however, they had often fucked right up against the glass, enjoying the view as they gaily violated one another.

During the warmer months they'd even frolicked on Peter's small balcony. The abundance of plants and flowers – Peter was quite the green thumb – providing a modicum of discretion in their manly endeavors. That being said, they still tried to keep their sounds of enjoyment somewhat muffled to avoid the unwanted attention of any neighbors who happened to also be on their balconies.

In his head, Alex had rehearsed the upcoming conversation a few hundred times and had worked out exactly what he wanted to say before they got naked. Amusingly, this turned out to be all for naught as Peter greeted him at the front door with an intense, fiery kiss and pulled Alex inside without saying a word. The kiss emptied his head of everything except the driving need to be in bed, with Peter firmly on top of him.

Wasting no time, the horny lads headed straight to the bedroom. Their clothes were hastily thrown into a messy pile on the floor, although Peter apparently did notice the underwear.

"These new?" Peter asked between frantic kisses.

"Aha," gasped Alex, as Peter bit hard into his neck.

"Nice. I'll fuck you in them later!"

And that was the end of their conversation, bar a series of loud grunts and moans. They were soon writhing together on the extra-large futon, sat in the center of the room. The kissing quickly progressed into a ravenous sixty-nine. Alex worked Peter's seven thick inches like the true cocksucker he was, savoring every morsel. The chemistry and craving between them was almost electric in its intensity.

Peter pulled back from his enthusiastic eating of Alex's juicy cock long enough to spit on his fingers and then roughly slide them inside Alex's tender passage, making the steward swear and cry out – albeit in a muffled fashion due to the size of the meat wedged in his mouth. The feel of the pilot's manly fingers spreading and widening his entrance was a familiar sensation that Alex couldn't get enough of, as he knew what was to follow.

A few heavenly minutes passed before Peter maneuvered down so that he could replace his fingers with his mouth. Soon he was munching away, working his tongue in and out, as he had many times before, much to Alex's joy. A thrill of excitement passed through Alex at thought of the hard hammering ahead. He considered Peter something of a power top and was a great fan of the pilot's manhood thrusting away inside him, usually quite brutally, well and truly owning his hole.

Evidently deciding that he'd given Alex enough of a warm up, Peter moved out from under him and reached over to the wooden box on the floor by the bed, which contained all the necessary supplies for fornication.

Alex promptly moved onto his hands and knees facing the window – doggy style was one of his most favorite ways to get fucked by Peter.

"That's a good boy, ready and raring to go," remarked Peter, his voice tinged with pride. "I've missed it."

His deep gravelly timbre turned Alex on even more, so he gave Peter an impish look over his shoulder and wriggled his ass, knowing full well the effect it would have. As expected, Peter was on the bed in a flash, his latex-covered cockhead nudging against the hairy opening and his hands firmly placed either side of Alex's hips.

Alex inhaled sharply as the cock stretched his sphincter and started to force its way inside. Thankfully, he had fully recovered from Simon's rough treatment but he nevertheless had to will himself to relax to let the invader deeper in, to fill him completely. Alex could feel each solid inch opening him up, making him groan in pleasure. He arched his back as he felt Peter's erection push in as far as it could go and holding it in place with his solid, powerful hips.

Peter paused only briefly and soon began to work the alluring ass with long, slow thrusts. Before too long, Peter picked up speed, holding tightly onto Alex in a vice-like grip as he pumped away. Droplets of sweat trickled down Peter's smooth, waxed muscles and dripped onto Alex's lower back as he reached a frantic tempo, pounding the plump ass before him.

The musky odor of Peter's perspiration drove Alex into a frenzy. He moaned louder and louder, squeezing his ass around the stiff rod impaling him. His hands scrunched the sheets as the waves of pleasure washed through his tensed body. Suddenly, Alex felt Peter's right hand wrapped around his cock, jacking it fast, driving him ever closer to climax.

All the pounding of his prostate had Alex pretty close to the threshold as is, but the sensation of the strong, rough hand pulling on his cock sent him flying over. Alex quivered as he shot a huge wad of cream over the bed and onto the floor. This was immediately followed by several spurts that fell on the royal-blue satin sheets beneath him, as Alex's overworked ass muscles involuntarily clamped down on the meat inside him.

Behind him Peter kept pumping but his ragged breathing and grunts signaled that an orgasm was only moments away. Peter gave Alex two more sharp thrusts before swearing and shuddering in release, filling the condom with his thick seed. He then lay down on Alex, pressing him against the damp, sticky sheets, while softly kissing the back of his neck and shoulders.

Alex turned his head around to the right so that he could kiss Peter affectionately on the lips. It had been a relatively quick play for them but seeing they both had the following day free Alex knew they had time to play again…and again. Alex still wanted to talk to Peter about their relationship but he was so blissed out after his release that he soon dozed off with the pilot wedged firmly inside him.

In fact, they both fell sound asleep locked into their delightfully snug position. They did move a few hours later when Peter briefly woke from his slumber, gently pulled out and discarded the condom before he maneuvered the sleeping Alex up to the top of the bed with his head resting on the pillows. Peter then pulled up the covers and cuddled Alex from behind, falling back asleep with his playmate in his arms.

* * *

The first to wake the following morning was Alex. He happily lay there in the warm cocoon of blankets, tranquilly wrapped up in Peter's strong arms. Indeed, Alex was content to stay right there for the whole day with Peter's morning wood pressing into his buttocks. He loved sleepovers and beginning the day with a friendly fumble between the sheets was always a welcome treat. Alex passed several minutes just enjoying the sensation of the muscular body encasing him when he noticed that the erection pushing into him had started to move. Figuring that Peter was waking up, Alex put his free arm behind him and onto Peter's firm ass to pull him in closer.

In response, Peter started kissing Alex's right ear and neck, while his hands began wandering over the hirsute body in front of him. His right hand grazed across Alex's erect nipples before traveling downwards, fingers raking through the thick furry covering of the torso and then instinctively latching onto the engorged manhood. Peter gave it a good couple of squeezes and then started stroking it gently.

Alex was keen to have the delightful dick inside of him again, so he reached forward to the wooden box and grabbed some protection. He passed it back to Peter who wasted no time suiting up. Alex's ass was still slick from the previous night, so the pilot spat on his hand to apply just a spot more lubrication before forcing his thick meat back inside the tight, but forever hospitable, passage.

Peter slipped in ever-so-slowly and took his time sliding in and out, making love rather than fucking. This was fairly standard practice for the duo after they had spent the night together, as both Alex and Peter enjoyed lazy morning sex. Alex was comforted by the familiarity of their play and felt his heart flutter a little.

It always feels so right.

A short while later Peter twisted around gently so that he was on his knees while Alex stayed in place. Alex cried out softly as the manhood rolled inside him. Once settled in this pose, Peter started to long-dick the velvety passage, withdrawing nearly all the way and then thrusting back into the base. Each time his hips pressed against Alex, the young cub gave a grunt of appreciation.

They stayed in this position for some minutes, enjoying the feel of each other's bodies. Peter then picked up Alex's right leg and used it to rotate him until Alex was on his back. Once he was lying flat, Peter spread Alex's legs wide and leant in to give him a deep, passionate kiss. Peter kept grinding into Alex, making slow, circular motions with his hips as they kissed. He gazed deeply into Alex's kind blue eyes as their tongues played together.

Feeling the weight of his muscular companion bearing down on him as they kept kissing, Alex was in heaven being stretched so wonderfully by Peter. He ran his nails down Peter's back, leaving small red lines in their wake – a little bit of pain mixed with so much sweet pleasure. The tender cocking caused a near constant stream of little groans and whimpers to escape Alex's parted lips.

The friends kept at it for some time, occasionally changing positions and sometimes not moving at all, simply resting with Peter's cock securely inside, but when they recommenced it was always with the same leisurely tempo.

After about an hour of this Alex was starting to get rather sore and his balls were in urgent need of release.

"Blow and breakfast?" suggested Alex.

"Your wish is my command."

If only you knew.

Peter eased Alex around onto his back again and increased his rhythm, pumping fast into the supple, round ass. He seemed in just as much need of unloading his full, heavy balls as Alex.

Alex gripped his cock and started jacking with gay abandon, desperate to explode. The powerful thrusts of the muscleman on top of him repeatedly hit his sweet spot and he could soon feel the familiar tingling in his balls. Only a few more thrusts later, Alex's body tensed up and he let out a series of sighs and grunts as he sprayed his seed all over himself.

The pilot kept pumping until Alex had stopped shooting, before he pulled out and ripped off the condom. He grabbed his cock and within ten strokes was adding his own cream to the load splashed over Alex's chest. Peter eagerly leant forward and kissed Alex, their semen mixing together in a tacky mess, matting Alex's curly brown chest hair.

Their lips remained locked in a loving embrace for a few minutes until Peter broke away.

"Now, let's see about that breakfast."

He hopped up and headed towards the bathroom to rinse off, leaving Alex to rest in bed. Peter was in and out rather quickly, drying himself thoroughly before he popped on his big, baby-blue dressing gown and going into the kitchen to prepare breakfast.

Eventually, Alex roused himself and went into the bathroom to freshen up. When he was done, dressed in Peter's other dressing gown – a short red robe that barely covered his privates – Alex wandered around to the kitchen and was greeted by the delicious smell of bacon and eggs, and freshly brewed coffee. Alex came up behind Peter, who was just finishing up the cooking, and hugged him from behind, giving the pilot's crotch a quick grope before sitting down at the glass dining table.

The whole scene felt very domestic and wonderfully comfortable to Alex.

"Peter…"

"Yes, handsome?"

Peter brought the plates to the table and set them down, looking at Alex expectantly.

Just tell him! I can't, I don't want to ruin this.

"Thanks for last night and this morning."

"Any time, my furry friend."

Peter smiled and Alex's heart melted a little more. Only slightly disappointed in himself, Alex tucked into his breakfast and the duo ate in companionable silence, as the sunlight poured in through the kitchen windows.

After breakfast they watched a spot of trashy TV – a rerun of Big Brother – to let their food settle before heading back to the bedroom for round two, which was followed by round three…and so on, until both of them were nearly red raw from the excessive friction. During their rest breaks, Peter told Alex about his holiday and showed him pictures of the arresting natural beauty of the place – in particular the hot surfer boys.

Alex finally toddled off home around nine pm that evening, as he had an early start the next day. Fortunately, George and Gus were out so Alex didn't need to invent an excuse for why he'd chickened out and not told Peter what he'd promised to. The day of play had worn him out and it wasn't too long before Alex climbed into bed, still thinking about the object of his affection – and not just because of the phantom sensation of Peter's cock in his thoroughly worked ass.

I'll tell him next time.

* * *

A few weeks passed, yet Alex still lacked the courage to broach the subject of a relationship with Peter. Each time they met up, Alex tried to get the words out but ended up filling his mouth with something else instead – not that Peter ever objected, mind you.

To take his mind off his cowardice, Alex turned his focus back to his career and the decision that he'd been mulling over for the last few months. He looked over the course descriptions and requirements one last time and finally registered for the training to make the switch over to Europe International. Opportunely, Sam also wanted to shake up his career and would be taking the course with him.

It turned out that the class was going to be fairly small in number; only fifteen flight attendants in all. Sam and Alex would also be the only men, not too surprising considering the usual gender ratio in their chosen profession. The training was structured to take place over three consecutive weeks and had both practical and theoretical components. There was a lot to learn, given all the scenarios that could arise when a plane is alone in the sky with nothing but ocean for miles and miles, and potentially hours away from help. It was a little overwhelming to think of all the possible disasters – onboard deaths, violent passengers, running out of booze…

Thankfully, there would always be an air marshal on board to help out in times of need, which reassured Alex greatly. As part of the course, they were to be given a series of short lectures with an air marshal to inform them about their responsibilities and to help answer any questions or concerns they may have.

On the morning of the first lecture, a tall, well-built man, who looked to be in his mid-thirties, walked into their classroom. He had russet-brown cropped hair, a neatly trimmed beard and dark seductive eyes.

"Good morning, my name's Robert Manning and I'm your air marshal for today," announced the handsome newcomer.

Alex was a little taken aback when he saw that the marshal was none other than a guy he'd had insanely good sex with at a sauna three months previously. His cock stirred slightly in his pants at the memory. The marshal appeared to recognize him as well but maintained his professional veneer, not looking overly much in Alex's direction.

In the break, Alex was sitting by himself in the courtyard of the training center, as Sam had gone to the bathroom. He was halfway through eating an apple when he noticed a shadow fall over him and looked up to see Robert standing over him.

"Good to see you again," said the marshal.

"You as well."

"Did you enjoy the lecture?"

"Yeah, it was interesting."

Their small talk was painfully stilted by the awkwardness between them that they were both struggling to overcome. It was Alex who finally addressed the pink elephant in the room.

"So, the sex was pretty damn hot!" stated Alex, his face holding a cheeky regard.

"Yeah I thought so, too." Robert smiled broadly. "You were one of the best I've had in a while."

"Thanks, same for you."

"I kicked myself that I didn't swap numbers with you. I wouldn't mind doing it again, if you're keen?"

Alex was flattered and his cock had started to strain the crotch of his jeans as Robert's deep, authoritative voice reminded him of their steamy session. Part of him desperately wanted to have a second bite of Robert's fruit – all eight juicy uncut inches of it – but his heart wasn't in agreement.

"I'd love to but I'm kinda seeing someone."

But am I really? Maybe I should play with Robert. Why don't I just talk to Peter?

"Sure, no problem. I totally understand." The disappointment was clear on Robert's face. "Here's my card anyway…if things change. Anyway, I should get going, see you around."

Robert left the courtyard, passing Sam, who'd apparently been looking on from the doorway with great interest.

"Did he just give you his card? Lucky bitch!" remarked Sam, upon seeing the business card in Alex's hand.

"We've met before."

"Do tell!"

Realizing he had no choice, Alex then proceeded to give him a blow-by-blow account of their previous interaction, which had Sam's crotch bulging, just as Alex's had, in next to no time.

"So are you going to see him again?" demanded Sam.

"I don't think so…I don't know…probably not."

Alex knew why he was being so hesitant. He needed to sort out his feelings for Peter.

"Why not? Actually, if you don't want him can I have him?" Sam's half-joking manner was betrayed by his lustful countenance.

"He's a person, not an old pair of pants."

"Geez, when did you get so sensitive?" Sam roughly tweaked Alex's left nipple, causing his friend to yelp. "Lighten up, boy!"

In retaliation, Alex slapped Sam's ass as hard as he could. Things soon degenerated with the lads groping and pinching one another, all the while giggling like naughty schoolboys.

They were interrupted by a stern voice coming from the entry to the courtyard.

"If you gentlemen are finished horsing around, it's time for your next class," said their theory teacher, Mrs. Cunningham, disapproval dripping from her matronly voice.

The thoroughly chastised lads quickly gathered their belongings and exited the courtyard, shamed into behaving like grownups.

* * *

Later that week, Alex and Sam found themselves in the heated Olympic-size pool inside the Europe Air center, awaiting their first water training session. The first task involved being placed in a capsule under the water and having to unbuckle their harness before breaking the safety glass and being able to float upwards to escape. Their instructor, Matt, both helped and hindered their training. His confident manner put them at ease but his boyish good looks had them thinking about things other than safety procedures. Matt was very attractive, with a mop of wavy brown hair, an athletically-lean build, tanned skin and inquisitive hazel eyes – altogether quite distracting. Not to mention his tight, yellow shorts that clung tantalizingly to his ample form.

Alex found the capsule a bit terrifying to start with, but soon adjusted and on the third time around he was practically like a fish…or more like an otter with all that body hair. Sam, however, had been restrained in far more awkward positions and was fine from the first attempt.

"That was fun!" exclaimed Sam, after making it back to the pool's edge.

"Figures that you'd like being locked in a harness," teased Alex.

"Like you don't." Sam countered cheekily and grinning like a fool.

While their instructor laughed and frequently flirted with the women in the group, the boys guessed in which team he planted his flag and had Matt pegged as gay pretty much straight away. The final confirmation came when Alex caught Matt openly staring at Sam's plump derriere in the pool. Admittedly, it was hard to avert your gaze from such a scrumptious sight…the material of his trousers clinging tightly to the round globes inside.

Once they were finished with the capsule they broke for afternoon tea, coming back half an hour later for the life raft training – getting in and out, and discovering all the sealed pockets and supplies. It would be fair to say that Alex wouldn't have minded being all wet and alone in the life raft with Matt and his mind drifted, more than a few times over the course of the session, as to what exactly he'd like to do to the safety instructor if they were stranded on a desert island together. Not that he'd forgotten Peter but it was hardly as if he was cheating either.

What's the harm in a little fantasy?

At the end of their session, Matt dismissed the class but asked Sam and Alex to stay behind.

"You did a great job today guys. I think you'll both do really well."

"Thanks, it helps to have a great instructor." Sam flirted shamelessly.

"Yeah, you helped a lot," added Alex.

It was obvious that Matt was hoping to get into either or both their pants and Alex was sorely tempted.

"So, how would you two like to go out for a drink tonight?"

"Sure, I'd love to!" answered Sam unsurprisingly.

Alex guessed that Sam would happily jump Matt right there by the side of the pool if he could. To be fair, Matt didn't look seem he would be particularly opposed to such an attack. Again it was an idea that certainly had appeal but Alex wasn't in the right headspace for it. Besides, due to miraculously matching schedules, he had been getting enough action from Peter of late to sate his carnal longings.

"I can't tonight, I've already got dinner plans."

This was in fact true, as he had a regular pizza night with George – and Gus now too seeing he'd 'officially' moved in the previous weekend – although it could have easily been fobbed off it he really wanted to. If anyone understood the allure of casual sex with handsome strangers it was George.

"That's a shame. Maybe another time?" suggested Matt, sounding a tad disappointed.

"That's OK. I'm sure we'll be able to have fun on our own." Sam gave Alex a sly wink.

They made their goodbyes and Alex headed off, looking forward to a quiet night in with his flat mates, munching on pizza and guzzling soft drinks – it was their diet cheat day, after all.

* * *

The rest of the training was over almost before they knew it and all that was left was for Alex and Sam to wait for their results, which they received by courier two weeks after their last class. Nervously, Alex and Sam had met up to open their envelopes together. They were both fairly certain they had passed but weren't sure of their exact results. Upon tearing open the envelopes they discovered their worry was for naught and that they'd scored quite highly for both their theoretical and practical components.

Alex noticed that Matt's comments on Sam's report commended him for his hard work and dedication to the task at hand. Judging by Sam's smirk, Alex knew what exactly had played a part in his glowing reviews.

Teacher's pet…doggy style, I imagine!

Included in the envelopes were their certificates and trial schedules. Europe Air was in the process of restructuring, so the newly certified lads would have to wait a month before their long-haul shifts would commence. The airline wanted to integrate the freshly trained staff slowly into the existing crews; by having them do one or two international flights, then back to domestic, gradually phasing the shorter routes out of their schedules. It was also caution on the airline's behalf, as they wanted to make sure the flight attendants had no problems transitioning into the new roles.

Neither Alex nor Sam was bothered by the delay, as they knew from chatting to the other flight attendants that the long-haul routes were much more demanding and tiring. Fortunately, the airline gave the employees a trial of three months on the new shifts to see if they liked them, with the option of returning to their previous roles. They wanted a happy – rather than bitter and resentful – workforce, after all.

Ryan wasn't interested in making the switch to Europe International and was understandably sad to see his friends leave.

"We'll still catch up with each other," reassured Alex, when they caught up for drinks to celebrate the results.

"Yeah, but it will suck with the different schedules," lamented Ryan.

"Don't worry, I'll make time to pound that pretty ass of yours... assuming that William ever leaves it alone," teased Sam, although there was a clear trace of envy in his words.

Alex had been proved correct about Ryan and William with the pair seeing each other on a regular basis. How Ryan wasn't constantly limping from riding that wonderfully over-sized manhood Alex didn't know.

"Aww, shucks I feel so special," joked Ryan.

The trio broke into peals of laughter and spent the rest of the night, sipping cocktails and perving on hot men – what could be better?

* * *

Life was good for Alex. Work had been fairly painless of late and he and Peter had been acting very much like a couple over the past few months – having regular sleepovers, spending lazy days wrapped up in each other's arms and going out for quiet dinners together. Indeed, Alex had been exceedingly happy when he'd gone to the gym for a quick workout by himself and the chatty receptionist had asked where his boyfriend was.

The more time he spent with Peter, the more Alex appreciated what an amazing guy he'd been lucky enough to find. It was more than just the physical companionship, as satisfying as that always tended to be. Whenever he watched Peter pottering about in the kitchen or attending to his garden on the balcony, Alex felt a warm glow course through his chest. He also adored the spirited debates they had, usually over films and books – although both agreed that Terry Pratchett was an absolute genius.

They had spent Christmas apart, choosing to be with their respective families instead. Happily, the pair had been reunited in time for the New Year, which they rang in whilst naked in Peter's bed, drunk on champagne and in the throes of ecstasy. Of course, they still hadn't had 'the talk' but things were going so well Alex wasn't even sure they needed to.

Do we really need to define what we have? What if it just makes things awkward? Best to enjoy what we have.

Things may have continued on in this manner if Alex hadn't accidentally run into Peter's cousin, Derek, at his local Tesco store, while out for his weekly grocery shop. They both went to reach for the last tube of Smokey Bacon Pringles on the bottom shelf, when they recognized one another.

"Hey Alex. How's it going?" greeted Derek cordially.

"Good. And you? How do you like living in London?"

"Oh, it's alright. So many guys though, it's hard to find one that wants more than just a quick play…although that's alright, too."

They laughed companionably together.

"I'm actually envious of PP getting to tap your fine ass. He's told me that you're an amazing fuck." Derek's eyes were full of undisguised interest.

"Thanks."

The unexpected compliment caught Alex off-guard. Naturally, he was flattered that Peter had described him like that, although he hadn't realized that the cousins were quite that close. He was also pleased by the attention that Derek was paying him but knew nothing would come of it, as Alex was hardly likely to bang his potential cousin-in-law.

"He said we should try and get together some time," remarked Derek.

This threw Alex completely. He was confused and more than a little upset.

"Um…sure," came his awkward reply.

"Great. I'll get PP to set it up. See you soon."

"Bye."

As Derek walked away, Alex could feel his face begin to heat with color and his anger building.

What sort of boyfriend pimps you out to his cousin? His hot cousin. That's not the point!

Leaving his half-full basket in the aisle he stormed out of the supermarket and headed home, with every intention of calling Robert, whose card he still hadn't managed to throw out and was sitting on his desk.

If he wants to share me, then there's plenty to go around and plenty who'd want it!

Minutes later he burst through his front door, which led straight into the lounge room. Alex was pulled up short when he saw that he'd walked in on a very intimate scene – Gus on his back on the coffee table, his legs in the air and George pumping away between them. Upon seeing Alex, George froze in place.

"Fuck...sorry Alex...we thought you'd be out longer," apologized George. "We'll go to our room."

Ordinarily, Alex might've been annoyed by the violation of their household agreement to keep things behind closed doors but his anger was clouding his mind. Suddenly, Alex had a far better idea.

"No, it's fine, stay there... actually why don't I join you?"

"Fine by me," replied George amiably. "OK for you Gus?"

"Of course! Get your furry butt over here!"

Alex ripped off his coat, t-shirt, shorts, underwear and boots in record time. He moved over and planted a fiery kiss on first George – who was still balls-deep in his boyfriend – and then Gus, as both reciprocated in kind.

A flurry of action followed, as Alex's anger turned him into a cock-crazed animal, feasting on their flesh – not that Gus and George appeared likely to object. It was almost two hours later when they finally lay together exhausted on the back on lounge, each a satisfied, sticky mess. The polished wooden floorboards were littered with empty condom packets and a heady aroma of manly release hung heavily in the air. Alex was cradled between the two mountains of muscle, each with their arms wrapped around him.

"Mmm…even better than I remember," murmured George, nuzzling into Alex's neck.

"Yeah, you're definitely one hot little fucker," reaffirmed Gus.

"Thanks guys, it was awesome for me, too."

Having had a much-needed boost to his self-confidence, Alex was feeling much better. As the glow of orgasm slowly faded, however, Alex realized that while he was no longer angry, he was a mess of other emotions. He felt slightly ashamed that he had used George and Gus to vent his frustration – although judging by their noises over the past few hours and the smiles currently plastered on their faces he was sure they didn't actually mind. Alex was annoyed at himself for acting so rashly and most of all he was sad that Peter wasn't apparently as serious about the relationship as he'd thought.

It was then that Alex had a most terrifying realization.

What if he never thought we were boyfriends at all?

* * *

Alex spent the next week studiously avoiding Peter by not answering his calls, or responding to his numerous messages, forgoing the gym and not visiting any of their usual haunts. He felt guilty about what he'd done with his flat mates despite not being certain if he was even in a relationship in the first place.

When did my life become a soap opera?

Alex understood that he had no one else to blame bar himself for his current predicament because he could have resolved the situation with a simple conversation any number of times over the last three months. As much as he feared Peter's possible rejection, Alex needed to know where he stood.

After a lot more worrying, and numerous imaginary conversations in his head, Alex decided to finally sack up and put his feelings out there and if Peter didn't want to pursue a relationship then he'd move on with his life.

So, the following Saturday, Alex summoned up all of his courage and called Peter to meet up for coffee at Happenstance. He figured if it went badly the fear of embarrassing himself by crying in public would keep his emotions in check until he got home.

Hopefully.

Alex was waiting in the café when Peter arrived, already midway through his second espresso, which only added to the air of nervousness he was projecting. They made small talk for a few minutes before Peter apparently couldn't take this nervous version of Alex any longer.

"OK, that's enough, Lex. There's obviously something the matter with you and I'm concerned. Are you going to tell me what's wrong or do I have to divine it?"

Disturbed by Peter's uncharacteristically gruff manner, Alex found himself struggling to formulate a response that didn't make him sound like a complete idiot. His stomach churned, as he despaired at his own cowardice.

Stop being such a pussy! What the hell am I waiting for? He knows that something's wrong, just tell him already!

"Nothing! I'm fine...I don't...what do you mean?"

What am I doing? Why did I even come here?

"You've ignored me all week and now you look like you're about to either cry or explode. Please tell me what's going on with you."

76

Alex took a deep breath knowing it was now or never. He stared directly into Peter's questioning eyes and laid himself bare.

"I want to be your boyfriend!"

The words came out all in a rush, while Alex desperately hoped that his face wasn't broadcasting the abject terror he was feeling.

Peter started to laugh, but quickly stopped, a frown creasing his brow.

"I'm sorry, I'm sorry. That's so not what I thought you were going to say. I was worried that you were pissed off at me for something."

"I was…but it wasn't…I don't know."

"That's all I've ever wanted from the first time we met, you doofus."

"Then why did you tell Derek he could fuck me?"

"What? Is that what he said?" A torrent of emotion rippled over Peter's features – confusion, shock and anger. "I only told him that it would be good for the three of us to catch up…for drinks or something."

"Oh! But I thought…"

The realization of his stupidity hit Alex like a sledgehammer. A wave of embarrassment swept over him, leaving him wishing he could miraculously undo his impetuous behavior.

Why didn't I just ask him?

"I'm such an idiot!" lamented Alex.

"Lucky you're so cute then."

"Watch it!" Alex playfully patted Peter on the arm but was then struck by a curious thought. "But, wait, if you still wanted for us to be together why didn't you say something?"

"Well, after you turned me down I decided to not bring it up again. I didn't want to make you uncomfortable and risk having you not be in my life. Lately, it seemed more and more like we were in a relationship and I didn't want to jinx it."

Peter leaned across the table and gave Alex a slow, loving kiss. He sat back down and took Alex's hands in his, his eyes clearly full of joy.

Relieved, Alex relaxed his facial muscles allowing a smile of happiness to take over. It felt like a great weight had been lifted and he silently berated himself for leaving it so long to tell Peter how he really felt.

"Now, how 'bout we get out of here and make it official?" suggested Peter, giving Alex a cheeky grin.

The newly formed couple hurried out of the café and was back at Peter's apartment ripping off each other's clothes within five minutes. A frenzied bout of lovemaking ensued with Peter tenderly topping Alex and then switching over to Alex riding Peter hard and fast. After they'd both cum, twice, they collapsed down to the bed, sticky and smiling.

"You've made me so happy, Lex," whispered Peter.

"You too, PP."

Peter whacked Alex hard on his exposed, and quite tender, behind.

"Ouch! Sorry…Petey?"

"Much better."

And with that Peter moved his head forward and gave Alex the gentlest of kisses.

* * *

The following month, Alex was finally scheduled for his first series of long-haul flights on the Singapore route. Sadly, both Peter and Sam were working on different routes, New York and Montreal respectively, so he would be working with all new people. Alex was a little nervous, but he knew that he'd be fine once he got into the swing of things.

The airline's plane of choice for such flights was the A380, which had a capacity of over five hundred people, mostly economy class. It was a lot more passengers than Alex was used to but he took it in his stride. Another difference was that the larger planes had 'family sections', which all the crew tried to avoid working in if possible. They were chock-full of babies, children and frustrated parents, and could be a veritable hell when the little demons set each other off in a tantrum domino effect. That being said, there were sometimes perks, such as encountering the occasional smoking hot DILF.

By his third international flight Alex was getting the hang of it, despite being more exhausted, as he found it hard to rest properly during the break in their thirteen-hour shift. This time, Alex had been assigned the horrible child friendly cabin and was dreading it until he caught sight of something that perked him right up – a harassed-looking father seated with his wife and two young children. The man had pleasing features and curly brown hair. He looked to be in his late-thirties but from what Alex could see he was definitely in good shape, with muscular arms and matching chest straining against the man's light-blue polo shirt.

While he went about his work, Alex allowed himself to naughtily daydream about the passenger. He was hornier than usual, as his new schedule had meant far less time with Peter and only his hand for release.

Fortunately, the pint-sized monsters in his section seemed to be relatively well behaved and Alex got through the first six hours without any major dramas. Even so, Alex was glad by the time they dimmed the cabin lights to encourage the passengers to sleep.

About thirty minutes later, Alex had already finished cleaning up the galley and was just passing time until it was time to feed the masses again in a few hours. His fellow flight attendants were resting in their private section, so Alex was left to his own devices. He was alone in the galley and flipping through a fitness magazine when in walked the dreamy DILF. Alex quickly put down the magazine and assumed his professional persona.

"What can I get for you, Sir?"

"I'd love a beer, thanks," ordered the man in an agreeable baritone.

Alex promptly went to the far cupboard, retrieved the beer and poured it into a plastic glass before handing the passenger his beverage. He was a little surprised when the DILF stayed to drink it in the galley rather than returning to his seat.

"So you're into the gym?" asked the DILF, pointing to the magazine Alex had been reading.

"Yeah, when I can."

Alex wasn't sure where this was leading but he figured chatting to an attractive man was a better way to pass the time than simply reading about them.

"I actually manage a gym back home, but I don't get to work out as often as I like," bemoaned the DILF.

"You're still in great shape, though."

As soon as the words were out of his mouth Alex regretted them and worried he'd crossed the line.

Stop flirting with the married man!

"Thanks, you, too. I'm David, by the way."

"Alex, nice to meet you."

Glad that David hadn't seemed to mind the compliment, Alex relaxed and began to enjoy the easy conversation. They continued to chat for a while about different training techniques and protein supplements – as gym-goers are wont to do. David soon finished his beer but appeared to be in no hurry to get back, undoubtedly happy to indulge in an adult conversation that didn't revolve around his kids. After ordering another beer, he leaned back against the counter, evidently settling in for a longer chat. Talk then turned to David's holiday and how he wished they could have gotten a babysitter so he and his wife could have had some time alone.

In an instant, Alex could tell where this was headed – a clichéd porn scenario if ever there was. David was hardly the first married man who'd expected that just because Alex was openly gay he would gladly get on his knees for any guy that wanted a warm hole. In fact, Alex would have been offended if he hadn't been thinking about doing just that since he'd seen David earlier.

Despite only playing with each other of late, he and Peter hadn't decided to be exclusive, so Alex was still free to explore other options. Admittedly, the prospect of a quick spot of relief with David certainly had its appeal. And, to be honest, Alex was interested to see how far the obviously frustrated father would go in search of release, although that didn't mean he was going to throw himself at him.

Nothing wrong with playing hard to get, after all.

They chatted for a little while longer and Alex noticed that David kept reaching down to adjust the crotch of his bone-white chinos far more often than one would have thought necessary. David asked for yet another beer, which Alex happily got for him, their fingers lightly touching when he handed over the plastic glass. Alex leaned back on the counter and noticed that David's adjusting had turned into lightly rubbing himself, an obvious yearning in his light-brown eyes. Alex decided to put the poor man out of his misery.

"Is there something else you need?" inquired Alex, trying to keep a straight face.

"Well…I could do with a good headjob." A peal of nervous laughter escaped from David's lips.

"Righty'o then."

Alex walked over, grabbed the beer from David and put it on the counter. He then grabbed David's hand and pulled him into the nearby toilet cubicle. David offered up no resistance nor made any effort to conceal how his cock was now tenting the front of his pants, apparently far too riled up and excited to care.

Locking the cubicle door behind him, Alex turned to face David. It was a snug fit but enough space for the job at hand. They were standing rather close and Alex could smell the beer on David's breath. Alex went to undo David's pants to get a mouthful of straight cock when David surprised him and went in for a kiss. It was rough and passionate and not at all what Alex expected. Alex locked eyes with David and saw only carnal lust, with no hint of shame.

The one or two married guys Alex had played with in the past had wanted to get their rocks off and rush away as fast as they could, trying to pretend that it didn't happen. Rarely, outside of porn, you got guys like David; that while straight for the most part, were still thoughtful enough to reciprocate.

They kissed furiously for a few minutes, their hands grasping at one another in desperate want. Mindful of their situation and time restraints, Alex reached down and undid first David's, then his own, pants to liberate the rock-hard members within. Once freed, Alex was pleased to see that David had a very similar cock to his own – thick, uncut and a satisfying eight inches in length.

Alex broke away from the embrace and maneuvered David around into a seated position on the closed toilet. Then Alex sunk to his knees, anxious to get a taste of that delicious dick. He nibbled on the chunky foreskin, kneading it gently with his teeth before running his tongue over the salty cockhead, licking away the flavorsome precum and preparing for the main meal. Slowly corkscrewing up and down the member with a practiced ease, Alex fondled David's hairy balls with his free hand, eliciting all sorts of pleasure-filled noises from the DILF.

David grabbed the back of Alex's head, clutching at the wavy chestnut hair, evidently loving the sensation of the hot mouth sliding up and down his shaft and milking his cock – what man wouldn't?

As he went about his merry toil, Alex breathed deeply of the pungent sweet odor of David's crotch. The neatly trimmed bush of hair lightly scratched his face as he moved up and down. Gripping the bottom of the shaft tightly, Alex gained speed, his head bobbing up and down at a furious pace. Alex soon gathered by the way David was squirming and sighing that he was on the brink of orgasm. Sure enough, five seconds later he received his creamy confirmation.

"I'm cumming," David whispered through clenched teeth, within seconds his body tensed up and his seed erupted into Alex's warm, welcoming mouth.

Ever the professional, Alex sucked it all down not wasting a single drop, his cumivore instincts in full force, plus, he didn't want to have to clean it up afterward. He relished the taste of David's cum as it hit the back of his throat and slid downwards into his hungry belly.

When he had sucked the last of the delicious creamy juice from David's member, Alex stood up and was preparing to do up his work pants when David stopped him by placing his hands on top the steward's.

"Not just yet," he commanded, his voice gruff with need.

Without hesitation, David leaned forward and took Alex's precum-smeared manhood into his moist mouth. He gagged a little at first but was soon taking the shaft deeper and deeper into his throat.

Alex was a little taken aback, although he suspected that this was far from the first time David had performed such a feat, as there wasn't even a hint of teeth. Recovering from his shock quickly, Alex started gently pumping his cock into the married man's eager mouth. Like David before him, it was only a few minutes before the load building in his balls was in need of release.

"I'm close," warned Alex.

David didn't heed the warning; apparently keen to repay the favor. Alex shuddered and gasped, as he gripped the back of David's head and discharged his weapon. To his credit, the DILF slurped down the flight attendant's load without a whisper of protest.

When he was done, David stood up and gave Alex another firm kiss. Alex delighted in the salty-sweet aftertaste of each other's cum swirling between their mouths.

"Thanks so much for that," gushed a clearly grateful David.

"Happy to oblige."

After they pulled up their pants and rearranged themselves, Alex opened the door a smidge to check if the coast was clear. Thankfully, it was empty, so they both hastily exited the cubicle and moved back to the galley.

David surprised Alex again by hanging around for a bit longer, finishing his drink and chatting. Half an hour passed before David went back to his seat, giving Alex a broad smile as he left. As Alex started the preparations for serving breakfast he began to feel a strange sense of unease. Despite his satisfaction from the unexpected encounter he was slightly bothered. It was the first time he had done anything sexual with someone other than Peter since they'd officially gotten together and Alex found himself questioning his actions. It wasn't that he thought Peter would mind but rather the opposite.

How would I feel if Petey had done the same? Do I want to be monogamous? Am I turning into an old married man?

Alex tried to push these troubling thoughts aside as he went about his work and only succeeded when it was time to wake his sleeping fellow crew members and get on with the morning service.

* * *

The issue continued to play on Alex's mind so when he got home again, Alex decided to talk it over with George, rather than Peter. Alex figured it would be better to discuss it with his boyfriend only after he'd worked out what it was that he wanted exactly. He didn't want to seem like a flaky queen who couldn't make up his mind or worse, a jealous harpy.

Originally, Alex planned on seeking Sam's advice, but thought better of it when he remembered that his friend's idea of monogamy consisted of only taking one cock at a time. Granted, he had held a similar view not too long ago but he still felt he needed a more balanced perspective.

And so, Alex was seated at his small kitchen table drinking a fresh pot of Russian Earl Grey, patiently awaiting George's sage advice after he'd explained his dilemma.

"Ah my little boy is growing up," tormented George lightheartedly.

Alex punched George's right shoulder in a brotherly fashion.

"Very funny. Now, tell me what you think."

"Well, I've had open and closed relationships, which both worked to varying degrees but it really depends on the people involved. What's right for one relationship isn't necessarily the best for another."

"I guess."

"Gus and I are monagamish. For the most part we just play with each other but when the occasion for something else presents itself we are open to it. Much like when you wickedly forced yourself on us a few weeks ago, you big brute." George teased his flat mate affectionately.

"I remember."

Even though he knew that George was joking, Alex blushed slightly at the memory. He had since confessed to his flat mates about what had led to his less than gentlemanly behavior, but both George and Gus had been nothing but sympathetic and hastened to reassure him that they weren't traumatized in the slightest. In fact, they had freely offered their services, if he ever found himself in need of such an outlet for his anger again – what are friends for?

"Do you still enjoy playing around with other boys?" asked George.

"Well, duh!" Alex rolled his eyes theatrically.

"OK then. Do you still want Peter to play with other guys?"

This question was much harder to answer. Alex paused while he considered the alternatives.

"Um…I don't know…thinking about it makes me feel a little jealous, but I can't tell him not to if I'm not prepared to do the same."

"Realistically, do you think you could?"

"I do love sex with him and it's not like he's not satisfying me…but I kinda like my freedom to play around too."

"The allure of the new and different," remarked George, with a knowing grin.

"Yup."

"Believe me I understand, but sometimes relationships are about compromise. You've got to work out what you want more and what Peter would be comfortable with as well."

"That's the thing, I just don't know," lamented Alex.

"Give yourself some time. This is your first proper relationship. I have no doubt that you'll work it out but you should probably tell Peter how you're feeling." George's voice radiated wisdom.

"I know. But what if he doesn't want what I want?"

George could plainly see Alex's worry on his face and hear it in the timbre of his voice.

"That's something you'll have to work out between the two of you. Remember I'm here if you need me. My door is always open...and my bed."

George erupted into a big, throaty laugh and Alex gave him another playful whack.

"Thanks. I really appreciate it."

"Any time, my furry little friend."

They sat drinking their tea until Gus came home from work, at which point George and he disappeared off to their bedroom, leaving Alex alone to think.

Am I ready to be a one-man man?

* * *

Around a week passed and Alex still hadn't decided what to do. He was committed to his relationship, and there was no doubt in his mind that Peter felt the same, although neither of them had mentioned the 'L' word yet. While Alex hadn't played with anyone else since the DILF, he knew that Peter and one of his co-pilots Zach – a similarly handsome hunk of muscle – had had some fun on their last trip to New York. When Peter had mentioned it casually in passing, Alex had just smiled and changed the subject. It hadn't made him insanely jealous but he wasn't completely comfortable with it either.

Why must I always be so damn indecisive?

Alex didn't know why he was so scared of openly communicating his feelings and vaguely considered the possibility of therapy to help him with the problem. He began to worry that he would end up damaging his relationship if he couldn't be honest and confide in Peter more often.

I don't want to lose him.

Strangely enough, it wasn't a therapist but a passenger on a flight back from Singapore that finally gave Alex the clarity he'd been seeking. The plane was over an hour away from Heathrow when they ran into a bad bout of turbulence. The seatbelt sign had been on for a good ten minutes and Alex himself was strapped into his jump seat near the main exit, as were the other attendants. The shaking began to subside and Alex hoped that they were through the worst of it. Despite flying regularly, he still got a little nervous whenever the turbulence rose above the occasional bump and jiggle.

Alex looked up over to Robert, who was sitting in front row of the middle section. He had been the marshal on a few of Alex's flights and they had long ago gotten past the awkwardness of having slept together. It helped that Robert was now happily dating Matt, Alex's previous water safety instructor, according to the airline grapevine at any rate.

Robert gave him a reassuring smile, apparently noticing Alex's unease at the turbulence. Alex felt slightly better but would be happier when the shaking had stopped completely and he could get back to work.

It was then that a portly gentleman, in the aisle seat four rows back, stood up and attempted to get something from the overhead compartment. Alex quickly unbuckled himself and moved towards the passenger.

"I'm sorry, Sir, but you must remain seated until the seatbelt sign has been switched off."

"Look, I just want to get my laptop. You just stick to mincing up and down handing out drinks," the passenger sneered.

Ignoring the extremely insulting comment, Alex took a deep breath and continued in his efforts to have the passenger obey safety protocol.

"Please, Sir. I must insist that you sit back do…"

The plane suddenly lurched quickly to the left and back again sending Alex off-balance. He fell forward and his hand caught on the rude passenger's arm.

"Don't fucking touch me, faggot!" he yelled, roughly shoving Alex to the side.

As he fell Alex could hear the gasps of the other passengers, presumably shocked, as he was, at this outrageous behavior. He only had a second to ponder this until his head smacked hard into the armrest of one of the seats on the opposite side of the aisle. Pain exploded through the right side of his head and he blacked out momentarily. When he came to, he saw the passenger being frog-marched by Robert, straight up the aisle towards the back of the plane. Alex could hear the concerned voices of passengers all around him and thought they were overreacting a little until he tentatively touched his face and felt the swelling around his right eye.

"Your poor face!" exclaimed Mary, a motherly, middle-aged brunette and one of his fellow cabin crew. "Can you stand?"

"I think so."

Alex used the offending armrest and Mary's hand for support and slowly climbed to his feet. The two other attendants from their section, Judy and Peta, soon joined them and together they slowly walked towards the galley. Mercifully, the turbulence had subsided quite substantially down to just the occasional shudder.

As they went, Alex heard his co-workers trying to reassure the other passengers and keep them calm.

"It's fine, everything is under control."

"No, thanks for the offer but it's best to say seated."

"Yes, I'll bring you a gin and tonic in a moment."

When they reached the galley, and pulled the curtain back behind them, Alex was pleased to see that the passenger was handcuffed and sitting in the corner with a very angry-looking Robert standing over him.

"I'll sue. This is illegal detainment!" protested the passenger.

Apparently, he hadn't quite grasped the seriousness of the situation. Mary sat Alex down on the far side of the galley, away from his attacker, and tended to his injuries, wrapping ice cubes in a thin bandage from the First Aid kit and placing it on his eye to help reduce the swelling. Judy and Peta had returned to the cabin to keep the rest of the passengers in check.

"I think you should sit there quietly and think about what you've done like a grown up," instructed Robert, his tone dark with barely contained rage.

"It's not my fault. The faggot shouldn't have grabbed me!"

This bigoted remark was obviously one too many and Robert snapped. He shoved the passenger forcefully back against the wall, making him to wince in response.

"Listen to me you homophobic little prick! You've attacked a member of the flight crew. Not only will you be brought up on an assault charge but they are liable to add terrorism or endangering an aircraft as well!"

Alex looked past Mary and saw the color drain from the pompous passenger's face. His head throbbed but the sight of the man being put in his place took the edge off – that and the rather strong painkiller Mary had given him.

"But I never…look I didn't mean…they can't…" the passenger stammered and started to sweat profusely. "I'm sorry, alright. It's all just a misunderstanding."

"Really? Because the swollen face of my co-worker says differently," continued Robert, obviously enjoying the discomfort he was causing.

The passenger then seemed at a loss for words and hung his head silently, radiating an aura of disgrace. By this time Mary had finished temporarily patching up Alex and then slowly led him back up the aisle to his seat.

"Looks like you'll have a nasty mark but you won't need stitches," comforted Mary.

"Pity, scars are sexy," he joked, trying to make the best of a bad situation.

"You rest here now, love. We'll be fine to finish the flight."

"You sure?"

"Positive." Mary said in her habitual calming tone. "Besides we can't have you fainting halfway up the aisle now, can we?"

"I guess not. Thanks."

"My pleasure, you poor dear. Rest easy."

Alex leaned back into his seat and closed his eyes. The throbbing in his head continued to fade and he felt quite floaty. The next thing he knew Mary was gently shaking his shoulder.

"Wake up, love. We've arrived. There's an ambulance waiting to take you to the hospital to check you out. And don't you worry that nasty piece of work has already been hauled off by the police."

"Thanks," slurred Alex groggily.

Mary and Peta helped him down the aisle and into the air bridge where a wheelchair was waiting for him. Alex began to protest feebly.

"No, I don't need…"

"Hush up. You've had a nasty knock to the head. Just do as we tell you."

Accepting defeat, Alex eased himself into the chair and began to relax again, but then started up at a sudden thought.

"Has anyone called Peter?"

"Yes, love. He'll meet you there," reassured Mary.

Alex sat back and allowed himself to be ferried to the waiting ambulance and onwards to the hospital. The ambulance officers examined him on the ride there but they didn't seem overly concerned. He was taken through emergency and seen by a doctor fairly promptly, who confirmed that besides some swelling and a painful-looking, black eye, Alex would be totally fine.

After the doctor completed his examination he allowed two police officers, one fresh-faced and eager and the other with a world-weary look about him, in to talk with Alex. They had come to interview him briefly about his part in the incident but they already had a fair idea of who was at fault given the unanimous testimonies of the nearby passengers and flight crew.

They were just finishing up when Peter rushed into the exam room.

"Lex! Are you OK? Your face! I'll kill him!"

"I'm fine, just a bit sore. And while it's a great offer, I think these gentlemen might mind."

Peter turned around and apparently registered the police presence for the first time and looked slightly stricken.

"That's alright, Sir. We completely understand, but we would appreciate if you could refrain from committing homicide," said the older of the officers with a friendly smirk.

Alex was grateful that they had a sense of humor.

"We'll let you get along home now," stated the younger officer. "And you'll be kept you informed as to the progress of the case."

"Thank you very much for everything," said Alex, genuinely appreciative of their efforts.

"Yes, thank you, officers!" Peter was very nearly gushing with gratitude.

The policemen then departed the room leaving the boys alone. Peter gazed at Alex, the relief at finding his boyfriend not overly injured evident in his thankful countenance.

"Are you in pain? Is there anything I can do?" queried Peter gently.

"No, the meds are working just fine and yes, please take me home."

"I don't think so Mister, you're coming home with me." Peter's firm instructive tone appealed greatly to Alex's submissive side. "I've already organized for the both of us to have some time off."

"Petey! You didn't have to do that."

"Yes I did! My heart damn well near stopped when I heard what happened and if you think I'm letting you out of my sight then you're sadly mistaken, young man."

Even though he was protesting, Alex loved how much care Peter was taking with him. In that instant, Alex realized that he didn't want to share Peter with anyone else. They checked out of the hospital and Peter drove him back to the apartment and tucked him safely into bed. The pain medication and events of the day combined to take their toll and Alex contently drifted off to sleep, happy in the knowledge that his boyfriend was tenderly watching over him.

I'm so lucky.

* * *

By the end of the week, Alex was feeling markedly better. The swelling had gone down after two days, although he still had a nasty black eye.

"You look like a thug!" Peter had teased.

He hadn't left Peter's apartment since they'd gotten home from the hospital and Peter had been playing nursemaid the entire time. He had reluctantly allowed Alex's friends to visit but had watched them warily to make sure that they didn't tire him out.

George and Gus had insisted on dropping by every day, his flat mates very much concerned for his welfare, although they could see that Peter was the veritable personification of the perfect partner. It amused Alex to see how protective both George and Gus each were of him and it made him happy to have all these beautiful men in his life.

It was on the Friday afternoon that Alex received word that the abusive passenger – Mr. Bernard Cummings – had agreed to a plea deal. In exchange for pleading guilty to misdemeanor assault and interference of duty, he received a suspended twelve-month sentence, a five thousand pound fine and was required to pay for any medical expenses Alex had accrued, as well as apologize personally for his actions. Alex believed that it was a fair outcome but Peter disagreed.

The couple were lying naked in bed together, with Alex wrapped up in Peter's well-developed arms.

"They should take him to the public square and flog him!" proclaimed Peter.

"That's a little too medieval but I appreciate the sentiment."

"No one touches my man unless he wants them to." Peter growled protectively and nuzzled in closer to Alex.

I'm probably not going to get a better opening.

All week, Alex had been searching for the right moment to broach the subject of their open relationship and now he'd been given the perfect opportunity.

"Umm...speaking of touching, I wanted to ask you something," mumbled Alex tentatively.

"Sure, I'll touch anything you like," said Peter, his voice heavy with lascivious glee.

He promptly reached under the covers and grabbed Alex's semi-erect manhood in his strong right hand.

"Ah," gasped Alex. "That feels great but it's not what I meant."

"So, I should let go?" Peter's offer wasn't particularly convincing.

"No, I never said that." Alex moved his hand under the covers as well and put it over Peter's keeping it right where it was. "How would you feel if it was to stay just us?"

"What? You mean for tonight?"

"No, I mean, what if it was just us every night?"

"Be monogamous?" Peter had a curious expression upon his face.

"Yeah...would you be OK with that? I know I'm hardly the poster boy for exclusivity but I thought that maybe we could try keeping things between us for a while."

On the outside Alex was the picture of calm but inside he was trembling like a frightened bunny...or rather an anxious baby bear-cub.

"What's brought this on then?" asked Peter in a gentle timbre.

"It's something I've been thinking about for a while. After what happened on the plane it made me realize that I don't want to share you with anyone. I want you all to myself, even if that does that sound ridiculously sappy and not at all like me."

"So it only took a knock to the head then?" teased Peter, although when he saw Alex's worried face he changed tack. "That's fine by me, my hairy little hottie. You're more than enough man for me."

Relief and happiness flooded through Alex as gave him a Peter a passionate kiss to seal their agreement.

"I love you, Petey."

"I love you too, Lex. Seeing we are being all open and honest about things, can I ask you a question too?"

"Sure!"

Alex had absolutely no idea what Peter had in mind but he was filled with a nervous excitement.

"Do you want to move in with me?"

"What?"

"Well it's not exactly fast, we've known each other for years and I've loved having you here all the time this week. I mean it would have been better if you weren't all injured but..."

Silencing his boyfriend with an amorous kiss, Alex then replied. "I'd love to! You'll have to help me break the news to George and Gus, though."

"I'm sure they'll understand."

"I don't know, they can be pretty possessive," joked Alex.

"We'll win them over." Peter assured his new flat mate confidently. "So, you want to christen your new bedroom?"

"Damn straight I do."

With that Peter jumped on top of Alex, careful of touching his healing face and tenderly planted a long, loving kiss on his boyfriend's lips. Alex didn't think he could possibly be any happier.

I could look up into those eyes forever...

PART TWO

A surge of contentment flowed through Alex's body as he admired the sun setting over London, watching it coat the city in a warm glow of vibrant pinks and oranges. To be fair, Alex's sense of fulfillment was more likely due to the fact that his husband was currently massaging his prostate at a pleasantly slow pace while they made love. It was five years to the day since they officially become a couple and it had been a wonderful ride. In fact, they had married on the very same date a mere two years later and the honeymoon showed no signs of ending.

Their Big Day had been perfect – a destination wedding on a private beach in a small coastal town in Spain, with a hundred or so of their nearest and dearest. They had even hired out several villas to accommodate the guests and the wedding celebrations had lasted an entire weekend. Alex's fellow steward, Sam, had eagerly offered to be their celebrant and had even taken a course to become certified especially just for them, although the irony of the perpetual bachelor performing the wedding rites was not lost upon him or the happy couple.

It was made even more special for Alex as his parents had finally overcome their prejudices and come to recognize him for who he was, rather than who they believed he should be. Indeed, when Alex's father had amazed him by welcoming his new son-in-law Peter to their family – something Alex would have considered nigh on impossible only a few years ago – there was barely a dry eye in the house.

It brought to an end Alex's long struggle for his parents' acceptance. While his parents were not complete religious zealots, their conservative views had seen many a harsh word exchanged in anger, not to mention a good deal of frustration and sadness. Alex was immensely grateful for their change of heart and knew that even when their relationship had been at its worst he had still had it better than some of his friends, who no longer had any contact at all with their families.

Alex was thoroughly devoted to his husband and judging by the way Peter doted on him in return it was clear that his beloved felt the same way. They had spent the entire day together – mostly in bed…what better way to spend an anniversary, after all?

The lovebirds had started the day off with more than a few glasses of champagne and a delicious breakfast of pancakes with fresh fruit, drizzled with melted white chocolate – which Peter faithfully prepared for them, as he had for each anniversary. They ate sporadically throughout the day to keep up their energy as their day of loving certainly burnt off a lot of calories. Both men were a little overwhelmed with the flood of messages, on social media and texts, congratulating them on their anniversary – whenever they managed to stop molesting one another long enough to bother checking their phones.

Coincidentally, the flower deliveries the couple had organized for each other – romantics that they were – happened to arrive at the same time. They were both dropped off by a fetching young man with low riding pants that bulged quite indecently in the front – so much so that Alex had had trouble keeping his eyes up when signing for the deliveries. He'd been briefly tempted to invite the lad in to see what other surprise packages he may be carrying but their days of playing around with others were long behind them. Their demanding flight schedules meant they barely had time for each other, let alone any extra-marital relations.

Having worked his way up the steward ranks, Alex now exclusively catered to the needs of the first class cabin for Europe International, with New York and Singapore as his main scheduled routes. Peter continued to pilot for the airline as well and between the two of them they earned quite a comfortable living – not the easiest of feats for Londoners.

Peter's ripped, bodybuilder frame worked in perfect rhythm with Alex's stockier build, as the pair dedicated their day to ravishing each other's bodies. They had varied back and forth between slow, sensual movements whilst gazing lovingly into each other's eyes and more frenzied fucking where the only thing to be seen was pure wanton lust.

Alex gripped the sheets tightly, as Peter's manhood continued to penetrate him. He adored how the weight of his husband's smooth, muscular body pushed down on him with every thrust. The air in the room was scented with the heady aroma of Peter's natural musk, which Alex happily inhaled while his husband unhurriedly pumped away. Admittedly, Alex was a little sore, as this was the fifth time Peter had claimed his husbandly right that day, but the pleasure far outweighed any discomfort.

"We're going to be late," murmured Peter, into Alex's ear, after glancing at the bedside clock.

He increased his tempo from a leisurely cocking to a much more urgent pounding, in a clear attempt to bring things to a rousing finish, although Alex's ensuing moans showed that he wasn't opposed to the change of pace. Barely ten seconds later Peter's body tensed up and he began to shake, joyfully crossing the threshold of orgasm and splashing his seed into Alex's velvety passage.

Alex felt the throbbing inside him and the pleasing sensation of receiving his husband's load. Peter collapsed down on top of Alex, pinning him to the bed, and gently kissed his neck and shoulders.

Once he recovered his breath, Peter moved back, pulling out of Alex before spinning him over onto his back. Alex took himself in hand and started to jerk his solid eight inches. In an effort to help Alex reach his own happy ending, Peter moved down to nibble on his husband's heavy ball sack while reaching up to tweak Alex's large, brown nipples. Peter then inserted two fingers back inside Alex's sensitive channel, using his spent cream as a handy lubricant. Alex groaned and tilted his head back against the bed, as Peter's helping hands went about their arousing labor.

The added stimulation worked a treat and Alex soon began to tremble violently before a spray of semen was released over his own hairy chest and stomach. Peter slowly slid back up Alex's body, sliding across the slick skin until he reached the top and tenderly kissed his husband, letting the stickiness dry between them as the sun went down and the room gradually became dark.

"Better start getting ready," instructed Peter, as he playfully slapped Alex on his exposed furry behind. "We don't want to lose the reservation. I didn't wait three months for that lobster for nothing."

"I'd rather just eat in." Alex cheekily made a grab for Peter's member.

Peter gently brushed him off and gave him a quick peck on the lips.

"You can have that for dessert later…if you're a good boy," promised Peter.

A mischievous grin played about Alex's lips.

"I always am!"

Through some hasty work they managed to get ready and were at the restaurant right on time, both looking rather dapper and very much like a couple in love. The rest of the evening passed by in a blur of good food and champagne, and ended with the gents naked in bed, holding each other in a warm, tender embrace.

* * *

Even though Alex and Peter were perfectly content with their life together, they had set in motion plans that would change their world irrevocably. In fact, they were almost ten weeks pregnant! Well, to be more precise, one of their dear friends, Fiona, was acting as a surrogate and carrying their future child for them. Fiona was quite the looker with long, curly blonde hair and radiant blue eyes, and was one of the most genuine and caring people they knew – as well as an unstoppable bundle of fun, who'd never met a cocktail she didn't like.

It wasn't a decision they had taken lightly and there had been a year or so of thoughtful debating whether or not fatherhood was truly for them. Financially, they were ready, as the mortgage on their apartment had been paid off two years previously and their savings had grown substantially in the interim. The only real concern had been if they were emotionally ready for the challenge of raising a child and the possibility of it negatively impacting their relationship. Eventually, the devoted duo decided that they had more than enough love for a child as well and were ready to take the daunting plunge into parenthood.

Alex had expected his parents to be a tad resistant to the idea, as they were still rather conservative in their outlook, despite their acceptance of his marriage. He was then pleasantly surprised when both of his parents expressed how thrilled they were at the prospect of more grandchildren. Alex's father, with his eyes glistening and tremendous smile on his face, had even given his son and Peter big congratulatory bear hugs. In retrospect, it wasn't completely shocking as his father already doted upon the children of Alex's brother and sister and appeared more than happy to add to his brood.

Unsurprisingly, Peter's family had been overwhelmingly supportive, due to their far more liberal upbringing. Amongst the couple's friends, however, the reaction had been more mixed, with some quite keen to be placed on the babysitting roster, while others jokingly bemoaned the fact that they would never see them any more. Alex and Peter hastened to reassure them that they were becoming fathers not moving to the moon or dying…queens can be so dramatic.

The couple did acknowledge that their world would change quite markedly but it was a change they were more than ready to embrace. Besides, they had six months to prepare before the big arrival; which was another reason why they had spent their anniversary pleasuring each other in bed, as no doubt their sex life would fall victim to the side effects of sleepless nights and the more pressing needs of parental duties.

This was not to say Alex had no reservations whatsoever. He'd been steadily making his way through the large stack of parenting books on the bedside table and had been quietly freaking out at the vast amount of sometimes highly contradictory information contained within them.

How am I not going to screw this child up completely?

Alex didn't want to bother Peter with his every little qualm so he chose to confide in his best friend, Dean, instead. The pair had become friends after a chance encounter on a flight several years back, before Alex had been happily committed, where Dean had brazenly seduced Alex in the galley to their mutual satisfaction. They had kept in touch and their friendship had continued to grow when Dean had moved to London three years beforehand, to the point that they now knew each other as well as their respective partners did, maybe even more so.

Dean sported blue, thick-framed glasses, which coupled with his shoulder-length, chestnut-brown locks gave him a whole bohemian-writer-chic vibe. It was quite an appropriate look, seeing that Dean wrote a popular blog – Oh The Homanity! – for the website of Man Up – a fashionable gay lifestyle magazine. He was also working on his first novel – a queer steampunk romance with lashings of discreet Victorian debauchery. His tall, lean frame had gained a good deal of muscle in the last year or so, courtesy of intensive gym sessions, which bestowed on Dean a much more mature appearance than his actual twenty-three years.

A few days after Alex's anniversary, he and Dean were sitting at a window table at Curiosity – their café of choice in the heart of Soho – where the mouthwatering smells of freshly brewed coffee and sweet, baked goods permeated the air. They'd been sipping piping-hot Mochaccinos, in an effort ward off the cold of the day, and lightheartedly discussing Dean's latest relationship dramas; nothing major, but his unconventional situation sometimes gave rise to extra tensions.

In actuality, Dean was in a throuple with a lovely couple of lads, Mac – a well-built medical student with messy red hair, hazel eyes, and smooth olive coloring – and Tom – an attractive, raven-haired graphic artist, with crystal-blue eyes and an alabaster complexion. Alex was sympathetic to Dean's situation and while he could see the appeal of having an extra body around the house, having one man to love was more than enough. That being said, Alex certainly wouldn't have minded seeing the throuple indulge in spot of steamy action.

Three heads are better than one!

Once their respective relationship gripes had been dispensed with, they moved on to Alex's feelings about giving up work once the baby was born, which were mixed to say the very least. Peter earned a great deal more than his husband, so it made sense that Alex be the one to stop working until the child was old enough for school. For the most part, Alex was ready to swap flying around the globe and being out all night drinking for trips to the playground and three am feeds, but there was still that last sliver of doubt that he'd lose himself in the all-consuming role of stay-at-home-dad.

"What if I become cut off from the civilized world and end up one of those parents that are incapable of discussing anything other than their child's sleep cycle and bowel movements?" fretted Alex.

"I seriously doubt that," Dean said reassuringly, "Although, I solemnly vow to slap you senseless if you do."

"Thanks, I appreciate that."

"Don't worry; I'll always be here to talk about the important things…cocks and Madonna."

The two broke into hearty peals of laughter, causing the heavy-set, elderly man seated at the table next to theirs, to look over at them with an annoyed expression upon his round, flushed face. Oblivious to their neighbor's chagrin, the pair continued on in their animated conversation. They spent a very pleasant few hours together, chatting and watching the crowds go by, in particular some of the more strapping specimens that passed…they may have been in committed relationships but they still had eyes for beauty.

* * *

Towards the end of that week, Alex and Peter met up with Fiona to go for their first ultrasound. All three were a little nervous but also enormously excited to have a proper look at their baby. The expectant fathers stood either side of Fiona in the largish cubicle at the clinic, each holding a hand, while the technician – a bookish-looking man in his late thirties – applied the gel before he ran the transducer over her stomach.

"Everything looks good here," observed the technician. "Oh…hold on a sec…"

"What's wrong?" demanded Alex, suddenly panicked.

"Nothing to worry about." The technician hastened to reassure them. "It just looks like it's going to be double the fun. There are two heartbeats. Congratulations, you're going to have twins."

"Twins?" asked Alex and Peter in unison.

"You're sure?" Fiona was undoubtedly a little concerned about what carrying two babies may end up doing to her body.

"Most definitely!" confirmed the technician.

Once over the shock, the trio began to revel in the surprising news. Alex could hardly believe that it was only four months since he and Peter had been at the clinic depositing their semen into the plastic cups. They had decided to mix their genetic material together and let their little soldiers fight it out amongst themselves…survival of the fittest and all that.

After a few months of preparation – both physical and emotional – Fiona had been ready for the insemination. Happily, fortune had smiled on them and, to their collective relief Fiona had fallen pregnant on the very first try. All three were well aware of the potential problems involved with the process from reading up online and from other members of their surrogacy support group. Cautionary tales of failed attempts and miscarriages had instilled a sense of wariness that somewhat tempered their excitement.

When they'd gotten the first positive pregnancy test – which had been shortly followed by a second and a third just to make sure – they had been literally jumping for joy in Fiona's apartment. They had, understandably, been reluctant to share the news, except with close friends and family, until after they'd successfully passed the first trimester in another few weeks.

The lads still didn't know which of them was the biological father but decided they would have blood tests after the babies were born. Not that it would make a difference to them emotionally but it would be handy to know in case of potential medical issues further down the track.

Words could barely express how grateful Alex and Peter each were that Fiona was doing this marvelously generous thing for them. Fiona would not be the biological mother, however, as they had chosen donor eggs from the fertility clinic's catalogue – a process that had lasted a few weeks as they'd taken time to agree on a suitable candidate. Apart from physical characteristics, they also needed a donor who wanted to keep the whole process open, with no anonymity, to make it easier for their child to explore their origins if they so chose when they were older. In the end, the prospective parents settled upon a lovely lass named Vanessa, whose china-blue eyes, brunette locks, and fair countenance had attracted their attention. After meeting Vanessa for coffee, where she easily won them over with her friendly nature and vibrant personality, Alex and Peter knew they had made the right decision.

For her part, Fiona had no great desire to have the responsibility of raising a child of her own, so was more than happy to only be the birth mother rather than the biological. Her career in journalism saw her traveling extensively for work – although that would change in the upcoming months as the pregnancy progressed – which wasn't always compatible with child rearing, and she was content with the direction her life had taken. Not to say, that Fiona wasn't interested in playing a role in the child's life, but much preferred the mantle of the fun, glamorous aunt.

"Rile them up and hand them back," she had often proclaimed proudly when talking of her interactions with others' children.

Fiona had first met the guys about four years prior, when they'd all been out partying at a Pride after-party. They'd gallantly saved her from the advances of a thoroughly unattractive and horribly drunk man who wouldn't accept defeat. The lads had taken it upon themselves to be her knights in shining armor – or body glitter as the case had been – and she'd been indebted to them ever since.

The delightful damsel had been out drowning her sorrows after a relationship breakdown and they were just the tonic she needed. Her love life had been a tad chaotic over the years but curiously ever since Fiona had fallen pregnant it was as if she'd been doused in pheromones. Men absolutely flocked to her. There was no one serious at present, as she was understandably hesitant to become involved with anyone until after the babies had been born. For now, Fiona simply enjoyed the interest, cheerfully soaking up the unexpected attention.

In a happy turn of events, Fiona lived in the building right next door to Alex and Peter, in a compact, stylishly decorated, one-bedroom apartment. She'd actually moved there a year before the trio had even met and somehow they'd never managed to cross paths. Their neighborly positioning meant that the gents tended not to be far away when help was required, especially when Fiona had a bizarre craving in the middle of the night – the past week it had been vanilla ice cream and pickled sardines. Thankfully, her morning sickness hadn't been too severe so far, with Fiona able to keep most things down, although even the faint odor of popcorn was apt to send her running to the bathroom – an unfortunate fact she'd discovered on her last two attempted visits to the cinema.

Following the ultrasound, the trio went out to dinner at Fiona's favorite restaurant – La Petite Grenouille – to celebrate.

"To two healthy, bouncing, bundles of joy," toasted Peter.

"And the speedy recovery of my beach body," added Fiona, only half-joking.

They happily clinked their glasses of sparkling, non-alcoholic cider together – they forwent champagne for Fiona's sake. A few hours later, the lads bade Fiona farewell at the door to her building and made their way home. When they were lying in bed together, preparing to go to sleep, Alex couldn't help but broach the subject of their unexpected news. Driven by insecurity, Alex wondered if he would be up to the challenge.

How on earth will we cope?

"Are you really OK, with it all?" asked Alex. "I mean two kids at once are going to be handful."

"Well, it wasn't part of the plan, but I think I'll be ready. I know you'll make a great father. It doesn't matter if it's one, two...or ten, we have the support of the people that count and most of all, we have each other...Daddy Lex."

Alex smiled contentedly at his husband's reassuring words and his amusing new nickname.

He always knows just what to say. I'm probably getting all worked up about absolutely nothing at all!

It was to this comforting thought that Alex drifted off to sleep imagining all the cute identical outfits he could dress their future children in.

* * *

The following Sunday morning found Alex and Peter standing before a solid, wooden door awaiting entry. The front door in question belonged to the apartment of Alex's former co-worker, Ryan, and his boyfriend, William. They lived only a short stroll away from Alex and Peter in a small, yet modern, apartment building right by the British Museum. The foursome was quite close, having been on a few holidays together over the past few years and catching up for brunch on the weekends when their schedules allowed, which was the reason for their visit today.

The lads had been together for almost as long as Alex and Peter but seemed in no hurry to race to the altar. Their relationship was also a great deal more open than Alex's, with a near constant stream of guys passing through their bed – something Alex was occasionally envious of, if he was to be honest. Not that he was bored of Peter by any means but he'd be lying if he said that he didn't have the odd fantasy about the feel of foreign flesh. And considering they had a child on the way their current arrangement was for the best.

Probably…no, definitely!

The door opened to reveal a fetching blond twink, who had an air of satisfaction lingering about him, with William and Ryan standing close behind. It wasn't hard to guess what had been going on with the trio before the gents' arrival. The blond acknowledged them with cheeky grin and blatantly checked them out before making his way to the elevator.

"Friend of yours?" asked Alex facetiously, after they'd passed into the apartment.

"Hunter? Yeah he's quite...fun to have around." Ryan's eyes twinkled mischievously.

"Very accommodating," supplied William, with a hearty chuckle.

Due to the warmth of the early spring day, the terrace doors were open, letting a pleasant breeze flow throughout the apartment. The air was scented with the results of William's earlier toils in the kitchen – opportunely he was just as capable there as he was in the bedroom. The large oak table in the dining room was already set up with a generous spread of pastries, jams, pancakes, bacon, scrambled eggs and, most importantly, a large jug of mimosas at the ready. Taking their places at the table, the friends continued their lighthearted conversation while they began to partake of the delectable-looking food before them.

"So, Hunter seemed...happy," teased Alex.

"Surprised he could still walk after playing with you pair," taunted Peter.

"Well, we gave it our best shot." Ryan remarked smugly.

"You should have seen what we were doing to him over this table." The look on William's face was one of delicious wickedness.

Both Alex and Peter stopped mid bite and looked down at their plates, unsure whether William was joking or not. Given Alex's knowledge of the pair it was a good bet that they had indeed plowed Hunter six ways to Sunday right where they were all currently sitting. The thought wasn't particularly unappealing to Alex.

If I was single…

"I was wondering why it smelt like bleach in here," quipped Alex.

The foursome broke into raucous laughter and continued the rest of the brunch in very good spirits indeed.

* * *

Two weeks later, spring was in full force with budding leaves on trees and a veritable kaleidoscope of flowers beginning to bloom about the city. Peter's horticultural handiwork on their balcony had been rewarded with an explosion of brightly-colored flowers and vibrant greenery, making for a most pleasant spot to sit and drink coffee of a morning. Alex always marveled at his husband's ability to cultivate, making it seem so easy, as he pottered about planting and pruning. Whenever Alex had turned his hand to such pursuits in the past it had always ended in disaster.

"Who can kill a cactus?" Peter had cried in horror, when he'd encountered Alex's attempt at gardening a few years back.

The sense of renewal in the air had encouraged Alex to indulge in a spot of spring-cleaning. Unfortunately, when he'd been rearranging the hall closet, Alex misjudged the weight of a box sitting on the top shelf and managed to wrench his back – it had been aching steadily ever since.

Alex had hoped that it would get better of its own accord by trying to rest it as much as possible, but working a flight to Singapore and back had only served to aggravate it. He knew he should do something about it but was unsure what would be the best remedy. The solution came to Alex while he was having coffee at Curiosity with Sam, who'd recently moved back from a two-year stint in New York. He had left not long after Alex and Peter's wedding, to take up a brand-new position training American recruits to Europe Air, who were expanding into the US domestic market.

"You look so uncomfortable," remarked Sam, obviously noticing Alex's stiff movements.

"Yeah, it's not getting any better," agreed Alex, wincing as reached forward to pick up his caramel Chai Latte.

"I had a great massage the other day, from a place near Covent Garden. The guy's name was Aaron and he gave me the best release."

"I bet he did." Alex raised his eyebrows in an accusingly arched manner.

"Well, we did do that later." Sam admitted while grinning like the proverbial Cheshire Cat. "But, honestly he's got healing hands."

"I'm not looking for a happy ending."

I don't need any temptations.

"Ha! Nah, he's not like that at all. We ran into each other at a bar afterwards and then we played. It was strictly professional during the massage. What do you have to lose?"

"I guess."

"Trust me, you'll be back doing cartwheels in no time."

"Yippee," enthused Alex sarcastically.

Alex had been unsure of the idea but by the end of their coffee date the nagging pain had decided for him, so Alex took Aaron's number and made an appointment for that very afternoon.

A couple of hours later, Alex was lying face down on the massage table, in nothing but a towel, waiting patiently for the arrival of the miracle masseur. The small, heated room smelled strongly of sandalwood and lavender, and with the soothing music of Enya playing softly through the speakers, Alex was already beginning to feel much more relaxed. So much so, that he was startled by the sound of the door opening, causing him to turn his head sharply, which in turn sent a teeth-clenching pain down the left side of his back. The grimace upon his face disappeared, however, when a Nordic-looking god of a man, walked into the room and introduced himself as Aaron. The masseur was kitted out in blue shorts that showed off his muscular legs and a tight white polo that displayed a hairy blond chest and quite a lot of gym work.

Well, I can certainly see why Sam was keen.

"OK, Alex, let's see if we can sort out this back of yours," said Aaron in a pleasant, even timbre.

Alex laid back flat on the bench and let Aaron get to work. His strong, yet soft, hands rapidly sought out all the knots and tension. It was rather painful to begin with but Alex knew that he'd probably have to suffer a little to get the result he wanted. After a while, Alex felt his back begin to unlock and the massage became much more enjoyable as the pain gradually faded away.

As he lay there enjoying the hands, Alex's mind began to wander imagining what else the masseur's digits might be good for. Predictably, his thoughts caused a swelling in his nether regions which was fine while he lying face down but Alex knew that he'd have to roll on his back at some point for Aaron to work the other side. Alex's pulse began to race at the embarrassment that awaited him if he wasn't able to get himself under control. Unfortunately, no matter what he thought about to try and dampen his erection – housework, dead kittens, that time he accidentally walked in on his grandmother getting out of the shower – it remained resolutely firm.

"Time to turn over," instructed Aaron.

Reluctantly, Alex rolled onto his back, his manhood noticeably tenting the towel. To his credit, Aaron didn't say a single word and carried on in a strictly professional manner. The stress and mortification of having Aaron see his erection passed and it mercifully began to subside on its own.

Twenty minutes later, Alex felt completely relaxed. He slowly sat up and tentatively twisted from side to side and was ever so relieved to find that he could move without even a twinge of pain.

"How you feeling?" inquired Aaron.

"Pretty great, actually. Sam was right about those hands of yours."

"I'm glad he's spreading the word."

"Don't worry, I'll happily be doing the same."

"Good to know." A warm, genuine smile graced Aaron's lips.

"Sorry about the…" Alex began awkwardly.

"Don't worry, it happens all the time," reassured Aaron.

I've really got to stop fantasizing.

Alex practically floated all the way home after the massage and was looking forward to a quiet night in with his husband to help work off some of the sexual energy that built up during his massage. Sadly, it wasn't to be as when Alex arrived home, he found Peter in their lounge room talking to his very distraught-looking cousin, Derek. His usually perfectly floppy blond hair was in a sorry state and his strong green eyes were stained with tears. It turned out that upon turning forty, Roger, Derek's boyfriend of four years, had decided to 'find himself', which apparently meant kicking out his boyfriend and attempting to fuck his way through the twink population of London. It had all the hallmarks of a mid-life crisis… complete with age-inappropriate wardrobe and fake tan.

Peter took Alex aside, presumably to ask a relatively big favor.

"I know that we're trying to spend as much alone time as we can before the babies' arrival but do you mind if Derek comes to stay with us for a little bit?" asked Peter softly. "He's really in a bad way."

For Alex it wasn't even a question, he adored the way Peter went out his way for others. Indeed, Peter's generosity and caring nature were some of his most beautiful traits and one of the many reasons why Alex loved his husband so dearly.

"Of course not, he's family," stated Alex matter-of-factly. "It's what you do when they're in need."

I guess there'll be no impromptu sex around the apartment for a while.

"And I'm sure he'll be back on his feet again well before our little bundles of joy make an appearance."

"Petey, it's fine, honestly."

They shared a quick kiss and cuddle before returning to the lounge room to break the happy news to Derek.

"Thanks guys, I really appreciate it," gushed Derek. "I'm sorry I'm such a mess."

"Nonsense. If you can't be a wreck with your family, then who else?" remarked Peter lightheartedly.

This elicited a small laugh from Derek, before he moved forward to give Peter, then Alex, a warm hug of gratitude.

"Seriously, you're welcome to stay here until you're ready to face the world again," added Alex magnanimously. "Besides, Roger is an asshole and was an absolute idiot to give you up."

"Thanks again, to both of you. I'll try not to be too much trouble."

Once Derek was settled in to the spare room, the gents retired to their bedroom for the evening, where Alex was finally able to release some of that pent-up sexual tension he accumulated earlier – even if they did have to make a concerted effort to be quiet, lest they disturb their unexpected houseguest.

* * *

Friday of the following week, Alex and Peter were headed out the wide, glass doors at the entrance of their apartment building, on their way out to dinner at their favorite Indian restaurant – Mumbai Sapphire. Just as they were exiting, the lads ran into their downstairs neighbors, Robert and Matt. The couple had moved into the building about three months previously and lived two floors below Alex, facing the other side with magnificent views over the city towards the Thames.

Even though neither Robert nor Matt still worked for the airlines, the two couples had remained close. The former air marshal and safety instructor had both given up their jobs to start a private security firm together – Eagle Eye Protection – which provided highly capable personnel to a mix of straight and gay venues around London. They prided themselves on having all their staff receive sufficient sensitivity training and negotiation tactics to help diffuse potentially violent situations with aggressively inebriated or otherwise agitated patrons.

Robert and Matt were both very supportive of the guys having children, although they harbored no desire to become fathers themselves, much preferring to be the indulgent uncle types, as they currently were to Matt's adorable three little nieces.

"How's everything going?" asked Peter.

"Great!" exclaimed Robert. "In fact we just scored the security contract for Damnation last week. Do you guys know it?"

It was a relatively new kink club that was the hottest spot in town for those looking for a nastier edge to the playtime. The main action was of a weekend but the management also hired out the space to various Masters and Mistresses to entertain their clients during the week.

"By reputation. I'm a bit too boring these days," grumbled Alex, only half-joking.

"Well, we get a handful of free passes if you guys ever want to spice things up," laughed Matt.

"May have to take you up on that!" said Peter good-humoredly.

"Oh really?" Alex was more than a little surprised by Peter's interest.

"Could be fun." Peter directed a lascivious wink at Alex.

"Yeah, we were there last weekend. It was just like being back in Berlin!" proclaimed Robert.

"God, some of the shows were so fucking hot! Then there was all the action downstairs…" Matt's face became flushed with the remembrance.

Alex knew that the pair weren't strictly monogamous, and hearing of their exploits sent a shiver of jealousy from his head down to his loins and back again.

I miss slutty nights out. Yes, but I have Peter and our marriage is worth more than all the anonymous sex I could possibly have. Who am I trying to convince?

Alex wasn't entirely successful in persuading himself of the virtue of monogamy but his husband interrupted his inner monologue.

"Sorry but we need to be off or we'll miss our reservation," announced Peter, taking a hold of Alex's hand.

"Catch up, soon?" asked Matt.

"Sure, how about dinner at ours next weekend?" offered Alex.

"Sounds great." Matt agreed with a friendly smile.

The two couples parted ways and as he walked hand-in-hand with his husband, Alex tried to shake the uneasy feeling, which had resurfaced.

I'm happy with the way things are. Aren't I?

* * *

The next morning, Alex was padding along the hallway on his way to the kitchen to fetch himself some breakfast. Peter had left early that morning to fly to Hong Kong and wouldn't be back for a few days, leaving Alex and Derek alone in the apartment. Not that Alex minded, he and Derek got along well enough and, to be honest, he'd barely noticed his houseguest's presence. Understandably, Derek wasn't his usual social self and had kept mostly to his room in the time he'd been there.

Passing the bathroom door, Alex noticed that it hadn't been shut properly and was standing slightly ajar. The sound of Derek singing to himself, as he showered, filtered into the hallway causing Alex to stop in his tracks. Through the steamy haze and the clear glass door of the shower, Alex could see Derek slowly soaping up his muscular body.

Damn he's hot!

Alex stood there watching for far longer than just an accidental glimpse. In his defense, the view was truly breathtaking. He'd forgotten just how stunning Derek's body was. The last time he'd seen it in all its glory was when they'd all gone on holiday to Spain two years beforehand. His mind was suddenly flooded with the remembrance of the day they'd visited a nudist beach in Sitges and Derek had come out of the ocean his body glistening wonderfully in the sun, in particular his plump manhood, which was swinging side to side and looking absolutely edible. His mouth began to salivate at the memory, although his current view was equally mouthwatering.

The white suds ran down Derek's tanned, well-developed back and over the perfectly formed globes of his ass, dripping down his powerful legs. The sight caused Alex's cock to awaken and the crotch of his pajama bottoms twitched as the manhood moved beneath the material. A swell of guilt rose through Alex's chest and he scurried off before Derek saw him.

He's your cousin! Only through marriage. Yes, but I still shouldn't have been looking! He probably left it open on purpose. OK, now I sound delusional.

As he pottered about the kitchen, preparing milky cereal for his breakfast, Alex continued to silently berate himself for his less-than-honorable actions. A short while later, Derek came into the kitchen in just a robe, thankfully Alex's erection had since subsided.

"Good morning, have a good sleep?" asked Derek, seeming a little brighter than he had been.

"Yeah, good and you?" Alex half-mumbled, feeling awfully ashamed.

"Fantastic. Slowly starting to feel more like my old self."

"That's great to hear. I should get ready, I'm meeting Dean for a coffee," said Alex, wolfing down the remainder of his breakfast and practically fleeing the room.

"Have a good day. I'll catch you later." Derek settled down at the kitchen nook to make some toast.

Getting ready in record time, Alex was out the door a mere ten minutes later. The prickly feeling of guilt stayed with Alex for most of the day. It didn't help that when he thought about what he'd done the image of Derek's slippery body kept racing back to the forefront of his mind, creating a cascade of impure thoughts.

I wonder what I'd be like to…Stop it! It was just a one off thing and I'll never do it again!

* * *

Around two weeks later, Alex and Fiona were happily installed on the sun drenched terrace of Happenstance. The pair had a standing weekly date for coffee and cake, both sharing a love of all things sweet. Mercifully, her nausea and odd aversion to popcorn had petered out a few weeks prior and Fiona now had no fear in munching away to her stomach's delight. They were midway through their cappuccinos and two generous helpings of a rather moist chocolate cake, when a late middle-aged woman, reeking of cheap perfume and stale cigarette smoke, suddenly came to a stop in front of their table.

"You should lay off the cake, love. You're getting a fat belly!" remarked the woman, somewhat unkindly.

Fiona instinctively looked down at her stomach, her left hand resting on it in a protective manner. She was a few weeks into her second trimester and was only just beginning to show.

"Hello, Mother," greeted Fiona coldly. "Alex, this is my mother, Dawn."

"Nice to meet you," said Alex politely.

"We'll see about that," replied Dawn dismissively.

Alex was genuinely surprised that the two were related, as the pair appeared nothing alike – both in personality and looks. Where Fiona was quite fair, blue-eyed and blonde, her mother had a much darker complexion with silver streaked hair and small, dark, mean eyes. Fiona hadn't really talked about her upbringing much but from the little she had revealed, Alex gathered it'd been somewhat bleak – raised by a single mother who had been difficult to get along with to say the least…he was beginning to see why.

"And I'm not fat, just pregnant," stated Fiona defiantly.

"Pregnant? And who's the father then?" Dawn demanded in a faintly menacing manner. "Not this nancy boy?"

Charming! How on earth did Fiona grow up to be so open-minded?

"The babies aren't mine so you aren't going to be a grandmother."

"What the hell do you mean, not yours?" Dawn screwed up her face in confusion.

"If you must know, I'm carrying twins for Alex and his husband."

"I raised you better than that my girl. Imagine! Having babies for a couple of poofters! What's the world coming to?"

Dawn's increasingly shrill voice carried across the terrace, attracting the stares of the other patrons. Her disgust was evident to all those in the vicinity. Alex bristled at her derogatory comments but didn't wish to cause an even bigger scene. He could see that Fiona was also struggling with her own barely restrained rage. It was hardly the first time Alex had encountered such blatant bigotry towards his sexuality but it had never before been directed towards his unborn children.

I don't want them to suffer. How can people still be so ignorant in this day and age? Are we doing the right thing?

"In my day, they bashed the perve…"

"That's enough! I think you should leave," interrupted Alex angrily.

"You stay out of this, faggot! You can't tell me leave me own daughter," hissed Dawn venomously.

"I want you to go!" shouted Fiona, her eyes wet with the beginning of tears.

"Fine then, don't come crying to me when it all goes pear-shaped!"

And with that the Dawn turned swiftly on her heel and angrily stomped off down the street, leaving a trail of her pungent scent in her wake.

"Don't worry, I wouldn't dream of it." Fiona called to the retreating back of her mother.

Alex put a comforting arm around a visibly distraught Fiona, all the while having a series of uncharitable thoughts about her mother.

And they say it's the gays that shouldn't raise kids!

"Bitch!" snarled Fiona through gritted teeth.

"Do you want to get out of here?" asked Alex softly.

"No dammit! That bigoted old witch has had enough of my time. I'll be damned if she's going to ruin the rest of this cake for me, too! In fact, I'm going to order another. Caramel cheesecake, this time!"

"And I think I'll join you, just for solidarity, of course."

"Of course," agreed Fiona, a small smile adorning her lips.

Alex was relieved to see Fiona smiling again and was glad that his own family relations had never been quite so strained. He was concerned for not just for her wellbeing but for that of the babies as well – undue stress isn't particularly conducive to a healthy pregnancy. The new desserts were soon placed on the table and they attacked their cakes with great gusto. As they ate, the pair talked of much more pleasant things and eventually left the café in a somewhat better mood. They then strolled back home together, arm in arm, enjoying the agreeable warmth of the late spring day.

* * *

That evening, Peter was staring at his husband with a look of shock and disgust. Alex had just finished recounting the encounter with Fiona's mother and Peter was understandably disturbed and outraged.

"That fucking bitch!" exploded Peter. "How dare she say that? She has no right. No right at all! What the fuck is wrong with people? So much damn ignorance and hate!"

"No arguments here."

"So, is Fiona OK?" asked Peter, his voice steeped in concern.

"Yeah, I think so, but I'm going to keep an even closer eye on her."

"That's a good idea."

"I still can't believe that Fiona could have been raised by that…that…" Alex was struggling for a word strong enough to convey his contempt.

"Harpy? Troll? Shrew? Harridan?"

"All of the above!"

The pair smiled at one another, pleased to find humor in an otherwise unpleasant situation.

"We should do something for Fiona though. Flowers? Dinner?" suggested Peter.

"She has been talking about trying that new spa near Oxford Circus," remarked Alex, remembering one of their recent conversations.

"Perfect. She definitely needs pampering after having to deal with that. Honestly, it's amazing that she's so well-adjusted and open-minded."

Alex smiled at the thoughtfulness of his husband. Once again, he appreciated his good fortune to be married to such a wonderful man.

"Good. I'll book it tomorrow."

"Now, what can I do to make you feel better?" A cheeky regard playing about Peter's countenance.

"I have a couple of ideas."

Alex moved forward to take his husband into a passionate embrace. A rush to the bedroom ensued and the hasty discarding of clothes soon followed, accompanied by a good deal of moaning and groaning – fortunately Derek was out for the evening. Their residual anger over the incident ended up leading to some of the roughest and hottest sex they'd ever had in a while. Alex rather liked Peter in fierce protector mode, ready to destroy any threat to his progeny or their carrier. The sweaty shenanigans helped them to clear the unpleasantness from their minds – temporarily at least.

Later, when they were lying in bed drifting off to sleep, Alex's thoughts drifted back to that afternoon and wondered about the future.

When will people stop being so cruel and judgmental?

* * *

Midway through the following week found Alex sitting in his former living room and catching up with Gus and George. The large windows were open and the flower-laden scents of spring from the nearby park were wafting into the apartment on a comfortably warm breeze. Alex was sipping his Earl Grey tea and munching on a sweet potato scone – a recipe handed down by George's grandmother and one Alex had become quite partial to when they'd lived together.

The apartment hadn't changed much in the years since he'd moved out, excepting for a seemingly endless parade of flat mates. Indeed, the lads had had a great deal of trouble in finding a fitting replacement for Alex, with a wide selection of colorful, but ultimately unsuitable, candidates passing through in his stead. From inconsiderate fellows who didn't understand the concept of cleaning or paying for bills, to the couple who'd had regular screaming matches at one another and finally a clumsy chain smoker who'd almost managed to burn the apartment down on three separate occasions.

This had, however, come to an end with the arrival of Gideon, whom the couple had met at Damnation where he was employed as a gogo dancer. After a hard night of partying, he'd come home with them and had moved in a few days later – much like Gus had come to live there in fact, although unlike Dean they didn't seem to be in a throuple.

"Glad you finally found someone decent to replace me. He seems lovely," commented Alex to his former flat mates.

"No one could ever replace you, my dear," said George, giving Alex a friendly pat on the shoulder. "But yes, he is."

"Not to mention talented." The grin of Gus' handsome face left no doubt as to which attributes he was referring.

Alex could definitely see the appeal, when he'd encountered Gideon at the front door, dressed only in a pair of small, red jocks, which showed off his lean body to perfection – not to mention the almost obscenely bulging pouch at the front. He also had a pleasing array of tattoos, including a monkey whose tail disappeared tantalizingly inside the underwear. Gideon had showed Alex to the boys in the living room and had then retreated off to his room. Alex hadn't failed to notice that that the back view was just as appealing as the front.

I definitely wouldn't mind seeing him dance…among other things.

"So how goes impending fatherhood?" inquired George.

"Not so bad."

The tone of Alex's voice conveyed far more confidence than he actually felt. He briefly considered telling them about the unpleasantness at the café the previous week, but he didn't feel like rehashing the nastiness of it all.

"Can't wait to be able to call you 'Daddy'!" taunted Gus, full of cheek.

"Careful, or you'll get a spanking," warned Alex halfheartedly.

In response, Gus jumped up off the lounge, turned around and presented his bare buttocks towards Alex, with a tantalizing glimpse of his low-hanging balls appearing between his muscular thighs. His former flat mate was still very much in the habit of parading about the apartment naked – and still looked damn fine doing it. It brought back all sorts of pleasant memories for Alex, which in turn created a stirring in his underwear.

"Don't point that thing at me, who knows where it's been!" heckled Alex.

At which all three broke into raucous laughter, which in turn drew Gideon out from his room and into the lounge room.

"Now, that's a fine view," remarked Gideon, clearly enjoying the arousing display. "Are you lads misbehaving again?"

"Certainly are!" Gus continued to wiggle his derriere in a provocative manner.

"Let me know if you need a hand with anything," offered Gideon, as he passed through on to the kitchen.

The blatant innuendo drove Alex's libido into overdrive with his mind flipping through all manner of carnal possibilities.

Fuck, how hot that foursome would be! George, Gus, Gideon...all those G-spots to play with. Stop it, I'm a married man! Yeah, but still a man!

Keeping his libidinous thoughts to himself, Alex stayed chatting for another hour or so before bidding his friends adieu and heading back towards home to meet up with Fiona and whisk her off to that much-needed spa appointment.

* * *

Near the end of May, Alex caught up with Ryan and Sam for a late lunch at Veni Vino Vici, an Italian tapas-wine bar not far from Holborn tube station. It had been a little while since the three of them had managed to coordinate an outing and they were determined to spend the afternoon eating, drinking and being merry. The lunch proved to be absolutely delicious – especially the bruschetta with grapes, honey, pine nuts and goat's cheese.

After their bellies were well and truly full, they decided to head up to Soho to visit Simon's new shop – Man-Sized. Alex's former trainee had recently quit working for Europe Express in favor of opening a store catering to the needs of gentlemen of a certain persuasion – so, mainly clothing and the occasional sex toy. Simon's parents had bankrolled him but he was already doing a roaring trade after only a few weeks. It no doubt helped that he was still boyishly handsome in his mid-twenties, coupled with a naturally flirtatious manner that was easily able to convince many a besotted gent to part with his hard-earned cash.

"Here's trouble!" cried Simon, his face lighting up at the entrance of his former coworkers.

After they'd dispensed with the obligatory hugs and kisses of greeting one another, Simon then proceeded to proudly show the trio about store. It was rather well laid out with racks of fashionable clothing lining the walls and a series of glass cabinets running down the center, displaying a good many items of interest to the boys. Opportunely, Simon insisted they all had staff discount on anything that caught their fancy.

"Are they on sale?" demanded Sam cheekily, gesturing to a few gym bunnies trying on revealing muscle tops at the back of the store.

Alex looked towards where Sam was pointing and a flicker of interest raced through his groin.

I wouldn't mind seeing if they fit me.

"Sadly not," remarked Simon grinning.

"Well, not here at any rate," commented Ryan with a conspiratorial wink, causing the foursome to laugh.

"The place looks great," said Alex with genuine enthusiasm.

"Yeah, I can certainly see myself draining my bank account here on a regular basis," added Sam.

"Me too!" agreed Ryan grinning.

Alex was excited to see that Simon carried his new favorite underwear brand – CocKed. Alex loved the fit and the way the material cradled his assets in a most appealing manner. He had quite the range at home – briefs, jockstraps and everything in between – but he could always do with more. A loyal devotee of about a year, Alex had only been able to order them online as no store in London bothered to stock them.

Until now!

Quite some time – and a not inconsiderable amount of money – later, they prepared to head off to the Friendly Society, a funky underground bar, for a cheeky bevy or several, telling Simon to come join them when he'd locked up for the day.

"Catch you then, lads," said Simon, a puckish smile crossing his lips and reaching his eyes.

After a brisk walk, the trio settled themselves in the main room, which had been cheerfully decorated with Barbies and a fake garden suspended from the ceiling – kitsch at its very best – and were sipping on some ridiculously strong cocktails. Needless to say, they were tipsy in next to no time. Initially, they had to raise their voices to be heard over the blaring music but as they became more inebriated it seemed less of an issue, all their senses becoming somewhat dampened.

Around an hour later, Simon turned up and quickly downed a few drinks in an apparent effort to catch up with the boys' buzzed state. A little twirl on the dance floor ensued, not that there was a great deal of room to move given how tiny the space was with all the other jolly dancers.

All that drinking began to take its toll and Alex ended up at the urinals, for the third time in the space of an hour, one hand on the wall to steady himself against the slight tilting of the world, as he went about his business. He became aware of someone pulling into the urinal next to his but didn't pay any attention until he heard a familiar voice.

"Damn, those drinks have a kick," commented Simon from beside him.

"Almost as lethal as the ones you make," teased Alex.

Instinctually, in his drunken state, Alex's gaze drifted across to the mammoth manhood Simon was holding in his hand.

Damn, it looks even bigger than I remember. Stop looking! I bet it'd feel great to ride it again. I'm happily married, I shouldn't think about that. But, imagine being tag-teamed by him and Derek!

Disturbed by his lustful thoughts, Alex quickly finished up and went to wash his hands.

"I'll see you out there," he called to Simon as he hastily exited the door.

Once back with Ryan and Sam, Alex tried to get back into the lighthearted mood but his mind was troubled. Fearful, that he may end up doing something he'd regret in a drunken stupor, Alex decided it best to remove himself from the path of temptation. He waited until Simon had returned before making his goodbyes.

"OK, sorry guys but I'm going to head off."

"No! You can't abandon us! It's too early!" exclaimed Sam melodramatically.

"You won't have many nights like this after the babies come," taunted Ryan, in an obvious attempt to keep Alex from departing.

That's probably true. But I don't want to risk fucking things up! Why does my cock have to be so damn demanding?

"Come on, stay." Simon placed an insistent hand on Alex's shoulder. "There's much more mischief to be had."

The pulsing in his underwear at Simon's touch convinced Alex that he should in fact leave before he lost of self-control. Besides, Peter was due back from Hong Kong the next morning and he didn't want to be hungover for the reunion.

"Nah, I gotta go. Have a fab night, boys!"

Alex gave his friends an apologetic smile, before he turned and climbed the stairs back up to street level and towards home. Determined to overcome his licentious urges, Alex concentrated his thoughts back towards his husband where they belonged. All through his brisk walk home, Alex imagined what he could do to atone for his less-than-faithful longings.

I'll give him a proper welcome back!

* * *

The following Wednesday, Dean and Alex were wandering around the musty-scented aisles of Bits and Bobs – a secondhand store in Shoreditch – looking through the boxes of old photos and postcards. It was a regular haunt for Alex as he had often come across few interesting additions for his collection; such was the case today, finding a few vintage cards from several European cities that he'd never even vaguely heard of.

"I find that I'm really fantasizing about and checking out other guys so much more lately," admitted Alex. "Especially Derek since I saw him in the shower."

"But you're not fucking them?"

"Well…no."

"So, what's the problem?" Dean's voice held a slight note of exasperation.

"I just feel like I'm still kinda being unfaithful somehow."

"Seriously?" demanded Dean incredulously.

"OK, I know…I know, I sound ridiculous."

"Got that right!" Dean smirked lightheartedly. "Come back to me when you actually have a real problem."

"Thanks for your support."

"Any time, my dear boy."

Moments later, apparently having a change of mind about Alex's predicament, Dean retook up the thread of the conversation.

"So, are you and Peter still having sex?"

"Yeah, of course!" said Alex defensively, before softening his attitude. "I mean not as much as we used to cause of work and Derek being in the apartment."

Temporarily stopping his perusal of the shelves, Dean turned to face Alex fully and adopted a serious regard.

"If you want my humble opinion, and I know you always do, I don't think that's what's really bothering you."

"Is that so, Dr. Freud? Let me guess, it's all about my mother!"

Sarcasm exuded from Alex's whole being, as he returned to rifle through the box of cards in front of him.

"I think it's the baby thing."

Dean's declaration caused Alex's fingers to pause in mid-air. He looked up at Dean inquiringly. It was not at all where he'd expected the conversation to lead and he shifted uncomfortably where he stood. Curious as to what Dean meant, Alex turned back to face his friend.

"Go on."

"You're going to become a full-time dad. That's a huge change and as excited as you are, there is probably also feeling of being trapped and you're looking for a release. We've already talked about how you're scared of fading away into domestic parental servitude and I think this is just an extension of that."

The statement resonated with Alex, so much so he was amazed that he hadn't been able to see it for himself. Dean could be awfully perceptive at times.

"Possibly...it does make sense, I guess," acknowledged Alex a little begrudgingly.

"Although you could also very well just be a horny slut," countered Dean laughing.

"You're such a comfort."

"I try. Besides, I've met Derek, if I'd seen him in the shower I would've wanted to do a lot more than think about banging him. On the bright side, he won't be there forever. You just need to control your rampaging desire until then, you dirty cockhound."

"Easier said than done." Alex muttered in his discontent.

Reacting to Alex's obvious distress, Dean moved forward and gave his best friend a reassuring hug. A gesture Alex very much appreciated and which helped to soothe his rising anxiety. They soon broke apart but Dean apparently wasn't finished with his efforts to bolster Alex's mood.

"You've been a good boy for what...five years now?" he questioned.

"Yeah. Not even a kiss out of place."

"Then, I honestly don't think you have anything to worry about. But I do think that talking to Peter about the baby stuff might help. It can't make things any worse."

"I guess…I promise I'll think about it."

Alex wasn't totally convinced. Even though, he recognized that he'd slipped back into his former bad habit of keeping things bottled up inside, Alex wasn't ready to broach the topic with his husband.

Petey is so excited. I'll just have to work it out on my own. He doesn't need any extra worry. It's not like I've done anything wrong…not yet anyway.

"So, we done here? I could definitely go for a nice big glass of wine!" pronounced Dean theatrically.

"Sure sounds good," agreed Alex, clutching his finds. "I'll just pay for these and we'll head back into Soho."

"Perfect."

Alex made his purchases and the pair was soon on their way back to spend the rest of their afternoon in a pleasant haze of sunshine and a good deal of rosé. That being said, no matter how much he drank or tried to ignore them, his niggling doubts continued to skulk around the back of Alex's consciousness.

Will I be a good dad? Can I keep it in my pants? Will I still have a life of my own?

* * *

Midway through June, on a rainy Sunday afternoon, Alex and Peter were lying on the couch together, watching reruns of The Golden Girls – classic comedy and a favorite for both of them.

"What about Nicolas?" suggested Peter.

They been discussing baby names off and on for the last few months but still weren't any closer to choosing anything. They'd also opted not to find out the sex of the babies, so it hadn't helped them to narrow the field.

"Isn't that the name of your hot French ex?"

Peter reluctantly nodded and Alex quickly vetoed the suggestion.

"Violette?" countered Alex.

"Only if you want her to sound like a Jane Austen heroine," quipped Peter. "Jasper?"

"Nope, I was bullied by one in primary school."

It was starting to become rather frustrating. They were usually so in sync that it had come as a surprise to both of them that their ideas differed so much in this respect. Of course, they had been bombarded with suggestions from well-meaning family and friends but they wanted to decide for themselves.

Taking Dean's advice, Alex had tried several times to bring up his anxieties about the upcoming changes but it never seemed liked the right moment. Happily, his wanton urges had calmed down somewhat after he and Peter had managed to have an entire weekend off together, when their schedules had aligned, which they'd used to pleasure each other senseless. It'd helped that Derek had coincidentally chosen that very same weekend to visit friends in Manchester. The freedom of being able to fuck all over their apartment had reinvigorated their sex life and this in turn had helped to settle Alex's troubled mind to some extent…but not completely.

I really should say something. But I don't want to make him worry as well. Maybe it'll all just work itself out.

"Prudence?" offered Alex. It had been the name of his favorite grandmother.

"Over my dead body," joked Peter.

"Cecil then!" yelled Alex, clearly exasperated.

Peter leaned forward and gave Alex a tender kiss, in an obvious attempt to calm his husband. Unsurprisingly, it worked. Any annoyance that Alex had been harboring suddenly melted away. It really was a most effective way of settling any disputes.

"Enough talk," commanded Peter as he got to his feet.

Grasping Alex tenderly by the hand, Peter led him off towards the bedroom. Luckily, they still had a few more months to make up their minds.

* * *

After finishing with their second sonogram, the months were flying by; Alex and Peter took Fiona out to celebrate at Grandma's Kitchen – an American style diner near Trafalgar Square that Fiona had developed a penchant for of late. All three were still a bit in a state of awe following the latest scan where they'd been able to see proper babies in the image as opposed to just an indistinguishable blob. They had, however, remained firm in their decision not to find out the sex of the babies until the birth, as their main concern was health rather than gender.

In regards to that important subject, the genetic tests and scan had revealed that everything was progressing normally and that the babies appeared to be very healthy indeed. The news had been very well received by the nervous dads-to-be from their doctor – Dr. Gillian Parker; a capable-looking women in her early thirties, with golden-brown eyes and brunette waves scraped up into her habitual loose chignon. Aside from being one of Fiona's oldest friends, she had been wonderfully helpful on their journey with her efficient, yet comforting, bedside manner. Her wife had given birth to a precious little girl the previous year, so she was rather sympathetic to those couples who had to go to a great deal of extra effort to conceive. Dr. Parker had also been marvelously obliging in guiding them through the surrogacy process.

As they were waiting in the foyer, a man on his way out accidentally bumped into Alex. He was handsome, in a bookish way, with curly hazelnut-brown hair and friendly brown eyes magnified by his round spectacles.

"I'm ever so sorry. I wasn't watching where I was going," apologized the man profusely.

"Owen?" exclaimed Fiona, a look of great surprise flashing upon her features.

"Fiona! Wow! It's been ages. You look amazing!" enthused Owen, his face lighting up.

"Pregnancy will do that." Fiona remarked with a sly smile.

"Oh...well that's...I didn't..." spluttered Owen, before regaining his composure. "I mean, congratulations!"

"The babies aren't mine though," teased Fiona.

"Babies? Umm...OK. That's...not yours?"

Owen appeared to be becoming more perplexed in the extreme. Apparently having finished with her fun, Fiona elaborated more fully for Owen.

"I'm carrying the babies for Alex and Peter, here."

It amused Alex to see both the way in which Fiona was joking with Owen and the subsequent look of relief that passed over his face when he learned the truth. The smallest inkling of an idea began to form.

"Pleased to meet you both," said Owen, offering his hand first to Alex then Peter.

"Owen and I used to work together at The Daily Messenger," explained Fiona, before turning her attention back to Owen. "Are you finished lunch?"

"No, actually. I was stood up for a blind date." Owen tilted his head down in a show of obvious embarrassment.

"Their loss, our gain," declared Fiona. "Won't you join us for lunch? If you boys don't mind?"

"Certainly," said Alex, his mind starting to turn with possibilities.

"We'd be delighted," added Peter.

Over the course of the next hour, the foursome passed a most lovely lunch together and Alex couldn't fail to notice the easy manner between Fiona and Owen, especially the way Owen seemed to hang upon her every word.

Later that evening, when he was snuggled up in Peter's strong arms, Alex had made up his mind. He was going to play matchmaker. Not only did he get to help a friend, but it also succeeded in turning his thoughts from his lingering fatherhood worries.

Fiona deserves to be happy; after all she's done for us. Owen is really charming...and already quite smitten unless I'm mistaken.

* * *

Determined to not waste any time, Alex put his plan into motion the following day during his and Fiona's regular coffee date. Fortunately, none of their recent get-togethers had suffered again from the intrusion of disgruntled family members. Annoyingly, they were deterred in their first choice by the overly packed terrace of Happenstance, due to everyone taking advantage of the exceedingly pleasant weather. So instead, the pair forsook their preferred café for another a few blocks away – La Cakerie. It was one they'd been to a few times before and while the coffee wasn't anything special, the cakes were truly spectacular. Indeed, their immensely popular prize dessert was the Piecakie – a pie-cake-cookie hybrid. It came in three different flavors, all of which were to die for…and given the obscene quantity of sugar contained within each bite, it was a very real possibility.

Comfortably seated in the smallish, jasmine-scented courtyard – courtesy of the inordinate amount of the flower growing around the walls – the friends were enjoying two helpings of the aforementioned calorific treats. They had just finished discussing Fiona's wonder over her ever-increasing bust line when Alex made his move.

"It was really lovely to meet Owen yesterday," mentioned Alex, with a forced air of casualness.

"Yeah, he's such a great guy. We used to have to have so much fun mucking around the newsroom."

"So, did you two ever…"

"Ever what?"

Alex wriggled his eyebrows suggestively which only served to elicit a laugh from Fiona.

"No! Of course not, you rude thing you!" exclaimed Fiona in mock outrage. "We're just friends."

Not to be deterred, Alex decided to press the matter further.

"Why not? Don't you find him attractive?"

"Well, yes but…I don't know. It just never came up. Why are you even asking?"

"He certainly appears to like you, missy."

"No. He's never said anything like…do you really think so?"

"If he'd been any more attentive yesterday he would have been in your lap," chortled Alex.

"Ha! I don't know. He's just a good friend. I've never really thought about him like that before. Besides he's not really my type."

"A loser with no prospects?" Alex did so love to tease Fiona lightheartedly.

"You're absolutely hilarious, you know that?" Fiona screwed up her face at her tormentor. "Anyway, it's hardly like I can start dating anyone now even if I wanted to."

"Why on earth not?" demanded Alex, refusing to accept defeat.

Fiona simply pointed at her noticeably rounded belly and gave Alex a bemused look.

"Granted, that could be an obstacle but Owen barely even noticed when he first saw you yesterday. Go on; ask him out for a coffee. What do you have to lose?"

"My pride?" retorted Fiona, with a look of quiet exasperation.

"You know I'm just going to harass you until you do."

"Fine!" Fiona had evidently been swayed to the cause. "I'll invite him out."

"That's all I ask."

Alex sat back in his seat with a regard of self-satisfaction and had another mouthful of cake.

"But, if it all goes pear-shaped then I'll be laying the blame solely on you."

The menace of Fiona's threat was somewhat softened by the bemused expression upon her face. Talk then turned to the progress of Fiona's upcoming article on the rise of surrogacy in the United Kingdom – a topic with which she was well acquainted. The surrogacy support group that they were a part of had also been a valuable source of information, most eager to speak of their experiences – Alex and Peter included.

* * *

The temperatures in London continued to climb steadily and by mid-July it appeared it might even be the hottest summer in decades. The clement weather seemed to have a positive effect on the inhabitants of the city with smiles abounding and a general feeling of optimism pervading even the most jaded of souls.

In another happy turn of events, Alex's matchmaking skills had been well and truly proved as Fiona and Owen had been dating for the past few weeks. Coffee had led to dinner the following night, which had been followed by several other such outings. Alex couldn't remember the last time he'd seen Fiona so cheerful – outside of drunken clubbing shenanigans that is.

On a steamy Wednesday evening, Alex and Derek were perched on bar stools at Rupert Street in Soho; cooling off with their fifth round of refreshing cocktails – well it was rather hot, after all. Peter had left that morning for Singapore and wouldn't be back for a few days, so it was just the two of them. Apart from seeking respite from the heat, the twosome was celebrating Derek having found a more permanent solution to his living arrangements. A work friend of Derek's had been through a similarly messy break-up and was desperately in need of a new flat mate to make up the rent. Consequently, Derek was due to move his belongings over on the following Sunday.

"To new beginnings," toasted Alex.

"And the support of family!" Derek chimed in.

The news had come as a relief to Alex, as he was glad to have at least one alluring distraction taken out of his immediate vicinity. Not that he had repeated his bathroom voyeurism but his libidinous thoughts hadn't exactly faded away either. The heat also had put him into a heightened state of arousal and the declining frequency of his and Peter's sex life wasn't helping matters any. Even the many quick bouts of self-pleasuring he was engaging in weren't satisfying enough.

It seemed that temptation abounded and try as he might Alex couldn't help himself from noticing and longing for what he knew he couldn't – and most definitely shouldn't – have. He had even tried burning off his excess energy with multiple trips to the gym; indeed, he was the fittest he'd ever been, but all to no avail. Granted the strapping, straining bodies that surrounded him in such places did little to dampen his ardor, particularly as his increasingly sculpted body had garnered its own share of newfound attention.

The pair had enjoyed a few good hours of drinking and admiring the skimpily clad attributes of the fellow patrons but now the crowd was starting thin out. The cocktails he'd consumed were making their presence known and Alex was starting to feel more than a little sleepy.

"It's getting late. Wanna head home?" asked Alex, slightly slurring his words.

"Sure. Good idea, I don't want to be hungover for work tomorrow," admitted Derek.

The thoroughly inebriated duo walked out of the bar together in a happy haze of alcohol and headed towards home. Just as they reached the end of Old Compton Street, Derek suddenly stopped dead in his tracks.

It took a few seconds for Alex to realize that Derek was no longer by his side and turned to find his houseguest staring openmouthed at a couple of amorous guys fervently kissing on the street corner. It took Alex a moment before he recognized one of the men as Derek's ex-boyfriend, Roger, and gathered that his companion – who looked to be a good deal younger – was his latest toyboy.

Quickly assessing the situation, Alex saw the potential for an ugly confrontation so he jumped into action mode, grabbing Derek by the arm, firmly steering him away from the display and around the corner back towards their apartment. Tears were streaming down Derek's face as they walked but he wasn't saying a word. Alex was genuinely concerned for him and was glad they didn't have far to travel.

"It's OK, we'll be home soon," reassured Alex.

In a matter of minutes, they were inside the apartment and Derek was sitting on the couch, his face a picture of misery. It was obvious that any healing he'd managed to do since the breakup had been undone in one fell swoop.

"Can I get you anything?" offered Alex.

Derek simply shook his head, so Alex sat down beside him, patiently waiting until he was ready to talk. After a few minutes of sitting quietly, Derek seemed to recover from the shock and his upset turned to anger.

"That bastard! He never wanted to kiss in public when we were together. He used to go on and on about gross public displays of affection and there he was carrying on like a fucking horny teenager!"

"Well, he was kissing one."

Derek laughed at Alex's snarkiness and his body began to relax, his anger clearly fading slightly.

"Plus his hair is thinning and he's put on weight," continued Alex. "You're well rid of him."

"Thanks for saying that." said Derek softly.

"My pleasure. Besides you'll find someone better who knows what he has instead of desperately chasing after his vanishing youth."

"Thanks. I really hope so."

"You will. What man wouldn't want someone like you?"

Derek's smile began to falter and his eyes glistened with the start of fresh tears so Alex moved forward to give him a big, strong bear hug that they held for a good minute. Derek's muscular body felt good pressed up against his and once again his thoughts dwelled in an inappropriate place. The alcohol coursing through his system wasn't doing him any favors.

Stop it! Stop thinking with your cock! Use the right head for a change.

When they pulled back apart Derek had a grateful expression on his face. Their faces were only a few inches apart when Derek suddenly moved forward and kissed Alex full on the lips.

Alex hesitated a fraction of a second before giving into the kiss, although it was a decision he instantly regretted. Recovering his senses, Alex broke away from their embrace and stood up away from the couch.

"No, we can't," insisted Alex. "I can't do this."

"I know…Alex, I'm so, so sorry. I shouldn't have done that. I don't even know what I was thinking. Please don't tell Peter," begged Derek. "You guys have been so good to me and I don't want to ruin things between us."

A whirlwind of thoughts raced through Alex's brain, leaving him feeling confused, distressed and, above all, guilty.

"I…I don't know."

"Please Alex, I've lost so much lately and I know what I did was wrong but I can't lose you guys too."

Derek appeared perilously close to tears again and his pleas tore at Alex's heart.

"I…I have to…I need to think about it."

Part of Alex knew he should come clean and tell Peter what had transpired, but on the other hand he didn't want to make Derek's situation worse. Not to mention the unsettling fact that he'd enjoyed kissing Derek far more than he cared to admit. It was all too much for him to deal with in his current state.

"I'll see you in the morning."

Alex scampered off to his bedroom and closing the door firmly behind him. Casting aside his clothes, Alex switched off the light and jumped into bed, his head abuzz with conflicting thoughts.

I can't lie to Petey. But Derek was just upset and he's already been through so much. Why did I kiss him back? I'm such an idiot! What should I do?

* * *

Alex spent a fitful night, his troubled thoughts invading his dreams, and awoke feeling lethargic and generally out-of-sorts. His first impulse was to call Dean but his best friend was on holidays with his boyfriends in Madrid and wouldn't be back for another week, and it wasn't a conversation he particularly wanted to have long-distance. So, the job fell to his next best confidants - Gus and George.

Getting ready in a rush, Alex made it out the door thirty minutes later without catching sight of Derek whose door was still shut.

Thank goodness! I couldn't face seeing him this morning...or for a while.

A brisk walk later, Alex found himself seated on the plush sofa in lounge room of his former apartment, absentmindedly twisting his wedding band around and around his finger as he recounted the previous night's events to the boys.

"So, what do you think?" asked Alex, fervently hoping the situation was far less dire than he imagined. "Should I tell Peter?"

"I think you should. Best to have everything out in the open. Besides, it's hardly like you set out to seduce Derek or him you, and you both stopped before it went too far. Peter's a sympathetic guy. I'm sure he'd understand," counseled George.

"Yeah, but I feel even worse because I have been fantasizing about Derek…and other guys. It doesn't help that our schedules have been a bit mismatched of late and with Derek there, we haven't had a lot of alone time."

"I dare say that's half of your problem right there," said George knowingly.

"Probably, although Dean thinks it's the stress of impending fatherhood making me extra riled up."

"And there's your other half."

"I don't agree," commented Gus, who'd been sitting quietly listening. "I don't think you should say anything. It'll make things worse for you, Peter and Derek. And it's probably only going to temporarily relieve your guilt. You could damage your relationship, and Peter and Derek's relationship, all over a silly kiss that meant nothing."

"Actually…he has a point," admitted George.

"Come on! You can't change sides like that. Now what I am supposed to do?" lamented Alex. "It seems like I'll be fucked no matter what I do. Why does everything have to be so damn complicated?"

"OK then, how would you feel if the situation was reversed?" asked George. "Would you want to know?"

"I…I…Maybe? I don't know."

Alex flopped miserably backwards into the lounge. He was starting to feel even worse than when he'd arrived.

They are supposed to be helping me, not making things more complicated! What am I going to do?

"I do think you should tell Peter how you're feeling about things regardless. Even if you don't mention the kiss," advised

151

George. "He's bound to understand your worry over becoming a dad, he's most likely going through it too. And for the sex thing, sometimes you need to sit down and just schedule time when you can be together, even if it seems a bit forced to begin with."

"How romantic! That's bound to fix everything!" Alex heard the nasty tone in his voice and immediately regretted it. "I'm sorry, that was uncalled for."

"It's OK, you're not yourself." George was apparently in a forgiving mood. "And, yes, it does kill the spontaneity but it might help you get back in sync. Look, Peter's a great guy and he loves you. I'm sure you two can work things out."

"And we're here to support you no matter what," declared Gus.

"I know and I really appreciate it. I don't mean to be such a whiny little cow. Guess I need to make up mind for myself and go with what feels right."

Feeling slightly more at ease, Alex went to bid the lads adieu. In response, they both moved forward and gave him a fantastically reassuring hug. Alex felt so calmed being held between them.

Maybe two husbands wouldn't be such a bad thing? Stop it! I'm having too much trouble trying to hold onto just the one.

After a little while, the lads released their grip, leaving Alex feeling a tad vulnerable as he left the apartment and proceeded on his way home. As he walked through the busy city streets, Alex barely acknowledged the crowds of people zipping past him, too firmly wrapped up in his own head, anxiously trying to decide upon the best course of action.

Have I ruined everything? How can I be a good dad when I can't even look after myself? What the hell am I going to do?

* * *

That weekend, Alex and Peter were restlessly roaming the twisted corridors of their local IKEA, ostensibly to look at furniture for their future nursery, but there was an air of bubbling tension between them. Granted, animosity between couples isn't an uncommon occurrence at this style of store with many a relationship coming close to ending over something as trifling as their partner's questionable choice of lounge cushions. This wasn't the case today, however, as the stress had already been building up long before they'd set foot into the Swedish store of wonders.

It wasn't over anything that had been said; rather, it was what hadn't been said. Alex had resolved to tell Peter the truth as soon as he'd returned home two days beforehand but upon seeing his husband his nerve had deserted him. The guilt was slowly eating away at Alex and it had consequently made him irritable and far less agreeable than his usual self. Derek was due to move out the next day and had unsurprisingly made himself quite scarce since the incident, only coming home to sleep and change clothes.

Peter had obviously noticed the increased tension but Alex had refused to admit anything was wrong despite his husband's repeated concerned questions. The couple has been getting progressively snarky towards each other as the shopping expedition progressed.

"That is fucking hideous!" declared Alex, whilst staring disdainfully at the turquoise photo frame Peter had picked up.

"Better than that god-awful gilded mirror you were looking at," griped Peter, while he absentmindedly stroked his jaw in a gesture of annoyance that Alex knew all too well.

"Whatever."

"OK, that's it. What is wrong?" The sternness began rising in Peter's tone. "You've been in a weird mood for days."

"Nothing," muttered Alex, as he went back to perusing the shelves, not that he even vaguely interested in shopping anymore.

Silence reigned between them for a good minute or so, both apparently heavy in thought.

"Have I done something wrong?" asked Peter tentatively.

The fact that Peter was beginning to blame himself only served to intensify Alex's gnawing sense of shame. His resolve to keep the secret began to falter and Alex felt the words of confession coming to his lips.

"No, of course not…it's not that…nothing. I'm just tired."

Just tell him! He deserves to know. Yeah, but not now, not here.

"It seems like it's more than that," stated Peter, an edge of suspicion in his words.

"Why can't you just believe what I say?" Alex could hear his voice rising in shrillness and volume but felt powerless to stop. "Must you question everything?"

"I do believe you. I'm just worried. I don't understand why you're so worked up. Where is this all coming from?"

"Just forget it! I don't feel like doing this anymore. I'm going home!"

And with that Alex stormed out of the store – via the long and winding path – leaving a bewildered-looking Peter, and more than a few interested onlookers, in his wake.

Twenty minutes later, Alex was sitting on a grimy wooden bench in a relatively empty tube station, waiting for next train, feeling frustrated and seething mad – angry at himself for picking a fight and not simply telling Peter the truth and equally angry at Derek for making him promise to not say anything in the first place.

Lost in his inner rage, Alex jumped a little when a gentle voice spoke from right next to him.

"I'm sorry…" Peter began.

"No, don't apologize. It's all on me. I was acting like a right idiot. I'm so sorry!"

"It's OK, Lex, couples fight," reassured Peter. "I still love you even when you are being a disagreeable little so-and-so."

"I love you too. Can we just forget about it?"

"That we can."

Peter moved forward to embrace Alex, which he gratefully accepted. In Peter's arms Alex felt safe and secure, his husband's fiercely masculine scent surrounding him. The familiar and comforting aroma triggered a new wave of guilt but once more Alex fought hard to suppress the urge to tell Peter everything.

Damn Derek! I can't keep lying. Petey deserves better.

* * *

It had been a week since his fight with Peter and the secret still weighed heavily on Alex. On the plus side, Derek had moved out on schedule and while Alex had been grateful that he was no longer faced with a daily reminder of his transgression, he was still struggling about whether or not to tell Peter the truth.

Knowing well the importance Peter placed on family, Alex was conflicted to say the least.

But what will he think of me? Will I ruin his relationship with Derek? Can he forgive me?

In order to help distract himself, Alex was currently on a shopping expedition with Fiona and her best friend, Katy. Fiona and Katy had been friends since high school and were similar in both looks and personality, so much so they had often been mistaken for sisters. Like Fiona, Katy had long, flowing blonde hair, sparkling blue eyes and a rather slinky build. Indeed, they had often borrowed outfits from each other's wardrobes – until the pregnancy at any rate...hence the reason for the shopping excursion.

Fiona urgently needed new maternity-wear, as she was rapidly outgrowing everything in her wardrobe.

"I need you with me so I don't just grab the first circus tent I see!" Fiona had pleaded on the phone to Alex the previous night.

The late July day wasn't uncomfortably warm, but the light breeze still provided much comfort to Fiona who was becoming increasingly sensitive to the heat as her pregnancy progressed. Playing the doting dad-to-be, Alex made sure that she was well hydrated and insisted on regular breaks for rest and refreshment. The trio was slowly making their way down Oxford Street, in amongst the masses, but after the first few hours of finding nothing but oversized dresses with floral prints and big satin bows all three were beginning to become more than a little discouraged.

"I swear if I see another cutesy, lace fringe, I'll scream," exclaimed Fiona.

"Right there with you," agreed Alex.

He hadn't realized that it would be so difficult finding attractive pregnancy attire. Granted, it had never really crossed his mind before, as he'd no reason to concern himself with such matters.

And I thought finding the right outfit for Pride was exhausting!

At Alex's insistence, they stopped for lunch in a small café just off of the main street, giving them the time to replenish their hungry stomachs and flagging spirits. Fiona loosened her sandals to give her slightly swollen ankles some relief.

"Anything, I can do?" inquired Alex, his voice brimming with concern.

"You can stop fussing over me like a Mother Hen," joked Fiona, although there was a tone of half-seriousness to her remark.

"I just want to make sure you're comfortable."

"And I appreciate it dearly, but I'm just pregnant, not an invalid."

"OK, OK. I can take a hint."

"Better than most men then," interjected Katy, causing both girls to laugh out loud.

Alex took the ribbing in good humor and the threesome enjoyed the rest of their meal with boosted morale. Once sated, they were preparing to head back into the fray when Alex spotted some potential outfits in the window of a cute little boutique – Get Up and Glow – a few stores down from the café.

As soon as they entered, the trio looked at each other with knowing grins – they had found the answers to their prayers. The boutique seemed to be full of ensembles that catered to pregnant fashionistas, and in a whole slew of fetching colors. The lady behind the counter, a stylish middle-aged brunette wearing tortoiseshell, librarian-frame glasses, came forward to assist the trio.

"Hi, I'm Ruth. How can I help you three?" she greeted them in a friendly manner.

"Everything looks so beautiful," gushed Fiona.

"Thank you, my dear."

"So different from everything else we've looked at today." Alex complimented genuinely.

"Yes, that's why I started this place. I had so much trouble finding anything remotely decent when I was expecting and it drove me batty! So, I decided it'd be easier to design my own and here we are. Now let's see what we can do for you."

After inquiring about Fiona's favorite colors, Ruth went to work plucking things from hangers and shelves for Fiona to try on.

Alex and Katy happily assumed butler duty, ferrying items back and forth to the change room. Fiona was very clearly having a wonderful time playing dress up, although there were a handful of times when she needed assistance getting in and out of certain dresses.

"I'm bulging everywhere these days," wailed Fiona mournfully.

"You look beautiful!" reassured Alex.

"For a whale."

"Yeah, but a glowing one." Alex quickly exited the cubicle when he saw Fiona's darkening face.

In all honesty, Fiona hadn't exactly piled on the pounds, as she was still fairly active and exercised daily…walking, swimming and regular yoga classes with Katy. Alex and Peter also liked to stroll in the park with her, when their schedules allowed – one big happy family-to-be. The guys had even generously paid for three months of Baby Boot Camp – a hardcore group class for new mothers – after Fiona had casually mentioned the idea in passing. It was the least they could do after the gift she was bestowing upon them.

Fiona ended up trying on pretty much everything in the shop and was clearly tempted to take one of everything, but, with the guiding hands of Alex and Katy, she narrowed the choice down to about ten must-have purchases.

"Thank you so much!" Fiona hugged Ruth warmly.

"My pleasure, my dear. Don't forget to tell any expectant friends!"

"We will, not to worry," agreed Fiona.

"Yeah, this place is fantastic!" Alex proclaimed with a joyful countenance.

To celebrate, the trio headed over to Curiosity in Soho to toast their victory with tea and cake. Fiona demolished her white chocolate cheesecake in an astonishingly quick amount of time and then proceeded to have one of Katy's pumpkin scones and half of Alex's custard tart – she was eating for three, after all.

After they had spent an enjoyable hour chatting – and gossiping about the latest scandalous behavior of their acquaintances – Katy rushed off to get ready for a date with her latest fling – a policeman with a rather big truncheon apparently.

Lucky lass! What is wrong with me? I need to stop thinking with my cock! It's gotten me into enough trouble of late.

Ever the gentleman, Alex then escorted Fiona, and her spoils, back home. As he wandered slowly back to his apartment next-door his good mood began to fade slightly, as the thought of Derek and the secret he was keeping came back to haunt him.

What on earth am I going to do?

* * *

Early the next week, Alex was on his way home from airport after having flown the New York route and back. He'd been delayed nearly two full days due to mechanical issues with the plane and then extreme weather had grounded all flights. Tiredness made him sink back into his seat of the taxi, his eyelids feeling heavier by the second. He had almost dozed off when the driver pulled up by his building, causing Alex to jerk awake. After paying, Alex wearily climbed out and made his way inside.

As he entered the apartment he noticed that the lights were off but there was a soft flicking radiance coming from the lounge room. He walked inside to find the room aglow with candles.

Did I miss an anniversary? Has a fuse blown? Did I forget to pay the electricity bill?

"Hey Handsome, glad you're home."

Peter took Alex into his arms and drew him into a long, passionate kiss. The kiss soon banished Alex's tiredness, as his body responded to the ardent embrace of his husband. Things looked to be headed towards the bedroom when Alex suddenly pulled away.

"I can't do this!" cried Alex

"What's wrong? You seemed into it? Too tired?"

"I was...it's not that. I...I..."

Alex's eyes began to shimmer as tears threatened to burst forth at any moment. The inner turmoil of the past few weeks came bubbling to the surface and began to overwhelm Alex completely.

"Lex, what's the matter? You're scaring me."

I have to tell him. He deserves to know what a lousy husband he has.

"I kissed Derek! I didn't mean for it to happen. We were both drunk and he was super emotional about running into Roger and it just happened. But, that's all that happened. And I've felt so guilty about it ever since but Derek made me promise not to tell and I didn't want to ruin your relationship with him as well. And now you're probably going to divorce me and take custody of the babies and I'll be left all alone like I deserve."

Once the babble of words stopped, Alex was at a loss. It felt good to have admitted everything but now he had no idea what would happen. He tentatively looked up at Peter, who was looking at him with a curious regard.

"Do you hate me?" Alex asked timidly.

"Come here." Peter pulled Alex into a big, strong bear hug. "Of course, I don't hate you, silly man."

Alex pulled away slightly to face his husband.

"But, why not?" demanded Alex, thoroughly confused over his husband's lax attitude.

"Well for starters, I already know about the kiss."

The admission stunned Alex into speechlessness – temporarily at least. His head spun with a myriad of questions that when he'd had a minute to process the information, flew out of his mouth in rapid succession.

"You do? But how? For how long? Weren't you angry? Why didn't you say anything? Were you just waiting to see how long until I'd crack?"

"So many questions."

With a slight laugh, Peter tenderly took Alex by the hand and led his still startled husband to the couch, where they sat down next to one other.

"Now, I've only known for a few days, just after you left actually. I knew something was up with you but I couldn't figure out what. I ended up asking Derek and he confessed everything straight away. And yes, I was really pissed off to start with, at him just as much as with you, but Derek told me how he'd pleaded with you not to say anything. It took me a little while to calm down but I managed to get past it. I love you and I'm in this for the long haul. I want you to feel like that you can talk to me about anything. Yes, it would've been better if you were honest from the start but I understand why you weren't. You do need to promise me that you'll come to me first, if there's ever another problem like that."

"I promise," swore Alex tearfully. "But how can you trust me again?"

"Because I know you and I know that you didn't set out to cheat on me. And I know you'd never willingly try and hurt me."

"But I've thought about being with other guys...a lot," admitted Alex, his face heated in shame.

"You doofus. Don't you think I check out other guys and fantasize from time to time?" A warm grin played about Peter's lips.

"Well...yeah I guess."

"It's perfectly natural, Lex. We're young and healthy; it'd be odd if we didn't have those urges. But if you were acting on it all the time, then we'd have a real problem." Peter leaned forward and gave Alex the gentlest of kisses. "I know that I haven't been as attentive to you of late because of work and I think that's something we both need to work on. Now, has anything else been bothering you?"

Time to man up! He needs to know.

"Actually, yes," confessed Alex. "I…I'm completely freaked out that I'm going to be a rubbish dad and that I'm in totally over my head."

"You think you're the only one?" inquired Peter softly. "I'm been having my own little bouts of anxiety over it but I didn't want to make you worry either. I guess we're both been more than a bit foolish then."

"You got that right."

With the tension eased the boys continued to speak about their insecurities and doubts about the future. They talked and talked over the next few hours from the couch to the dinner table – to eat the delicious dinner Peter had prepared – until finally they had said enough and retired to the bedroom. After lovingly undressing one another, the couple fell to the bed and their bodies came together in the most passionate display that they had managed in months.

That night, Alex fell into a deep contented slumber, his months of worry cast aside and only thoughts of the happy things to come dancing about in his head.

How did I ever get so lucky?

* * *

Since their heart-to-heart, things between Alex and Peter had never been better. They had both made a concerted effort to make time for one another with a regular date night, which always ended up in a sweaty mess of limbs somewhere in the apartment – with Derek gone they were able to once again free to fornicate wherever they chose.

On a pleasantly warm evening in the middle of September, the pair found themselves standing amongst an eclectic crowd in the middle of Matt and Robert's living room to celebrate the latter's fortieth birthday. It was an interesting mix of people but they seemed to be mingling well enough.

After the party had been going for a few good hours, Matt stood in the center of the room with Robert by his side. Raising his champagne glass, he began to tap repeatedly on the side to draw the attention of their guests.

"I'd like to thank you all for coming to help Robert through this oh so difficult time," he joked, which sent a ripple of laughter through the crowd. "But seriously, we both really appreciate your presence and of course, your presents! Although we may have slightly misled you, as tonight isn't just about Robert's birthday. We'd also like to make a very special announcement."

They were a few confused looks about the place as no one but the hosts seemed to know what was happening. Alex looked at Robert questioningly but he merely shrugged his shoulders in response.

After taking a moment for dramatic pause, the boys proceeded to announce in unison.

"We're engaged!"

There was another brief pause of a few seconds, as the news took time to sink in, before there was a rousing round of applause and people rushed forward to congratulate the happy couple. Admittedly, the pronouncement hadn't been completely shocking for those in attendance, as anyone who had spent even a little time with the couple could easily see that they were very much in love. The party continued on in an even more lively fashion following the joyous news.

Fiona sipped on her mango-flavored mocktail as she chatted to Alex on the balcony overlooking the twinkling city nights. She had accompanied the boys solo – not including her two passengers – as Owen was away on assignment. Owen had practically been a saint as the pregnancy progressed, seeming almost as invested in the health and wellbeing of Fiona and the babies as Alex and Peter were. That being said, he was very much of a similar mindset to Fiona, in the respect that he was fond of children, from a distance, and was more than happy to simply borrow them on occasion rather than having them around on a full-time basis. Fiona had told Alex that they were content to take things slow until after she'd recovered from the birth.

Alex and Fiona were in deep conversation about Katy's new man – a strapping sailor this time – when she suddenly stopped mid-sentence and rubbed her stomach. Noticing an odd look pass over Fiona's face, Alex was immediately concerned.

"Are you feeling alright?"

"Umm…actually no. I feel a little weird."

"Come sit down." Alex directed her to a nearby chair with a calmness that belied the rising panic he was feeling.

It's too early for labor! What'll we do? Should I call an ambulance?

"Can I get you anything?" asked Alex kindly.

"No…I…I think I just need to sit down."

Once she was seated comfortably, Alex quickly raced off to find Peter who was fortunately only in the next room. They were back by her side in moments, both feeling understandably freaked out.

"How are you feeling?" inquired Peter, his face betraying his deep concern.

"The same…just a…strange feeling in my stomach."

"Excuse me. Sorry for eavesdropping, but can I help?" offered a fellow partygoer.

It was Robert's cousin, Dr. Samantha Meadows, a sturdy woman in her late fifties with strong dark features and an air of authority. She also happened to be a gynecologist of some standing.

"Samantha! Yes, please. I'm sorry I didn't even think to get you," exclaimed Alex, cursing himself for his idiocy.

"OK, let me see what we're dealing with."

With a capable manner, she quickly assessed Fiona's situation, taking her pulse and noting the symptoms. Her examination lasted only a few minutes but it felt far longer to Alex and Peter, who were nervously hovering nearby.

"Now, now. No need to panic. It appears to be a mild case of indigestion but I'll just pop downstairs to grab my medical kit from the car just to double check," reassured Dr. Meadows.

After she'd departed, Alex and Peter stood awkwardly by Fiona, unsure of what to say or do.

"Too many hors-d'oeurves," joked Fiona, trying to relieve the tension.

Alex and Peter exchanged a worried glance but did their best to support Fiona.

"I'm sure that's all it is," said Alex soothingly.

"Maybe the bubs are just being fussy." Robert's tight smile betrayed his deeper concern.

Dr. Meadows returned within a few minutes and proceeded to check Fiona's blood pressure and temperature, which seemed to agree with her initial diagnosis. She gave Fiona an antacid and after twenty minutes of resting the discomfort had all but disappeared, much to the trio's relief.

"Well, my work here is done," remarked Dr. Meadows with a confident smile.

"Thanks, so much," gushed Alex, his heart a mess of emotions.

"Yes, thank you, Samantha." Fiona gave her a warm regard of gratitude. "You've been amazing."

"Thank you, truly," echoed Peter.

"My pleasure. You take care now," said Dr. Meadows, before wandering off to enjoy the rest of the party.

"I think I may head home and get some more rest," announced Fiona, standing from her seat.

"We're coming with you," stated Alex.

"No, it's OK. I can manage. It is just next door, after all."

"That may be, but we aren't taking any chances," Peter asserted firmly.

"Fine, fine," agreed Fiona in a show of reluctant defeat.

The trio bid adieu to their hosts and congratulated them once more on the birthday and engagement joy. They rode downstairs in the elevator and walked the twenty meters to Fiona's neighboring apartment complex. Alex and Peter insisted on accompanying her all the way to her front door.

Despite her initial protests, Alex suspected that their protective escort secretly relieved Fiona.

"See you tomorrow for brunch?" asked Fiona.

"Wouldn't miss it," said Alex with an enthusiastic smile.

"Sleep well." Peter added as he gave her a warm hug goodbye.

Once they were certain she was safe and secure, the papas-to-be returned to their apartment building and were soon climbing into bed themselves, fatigued after all the worry. They were trying their best not to be over-protective but it was a period of adjustment for all three of them.

"I don't know what I would have done if it was something serious," lamented Alex, as he snuggled back into Peter's strong, naked embrace.

"But it wasn't. She's fine, the babies are fine."

"I know...but I still worry."

"So do I, but we just need to stay positive. Besides we have each other no matter what and we can handle anything that comes our way."

Alex pulled Peter in even tighter, which helped to lessen his fears and calmed him down further.

"Thanks. I needed to hear that."

Sleep eventually came, but those niggling doubts wove their ways into his dreams leading to a very unsettled night indeed.

* * *

A little over two weeks later, the expectant trio was filled with a sense of renewed assurance, as they'd dispensed with the third sonogram, which had thankfully given them the all clear. It would be fair to say that after the scare at the engagement party, they'd all been a little on edge. Even though they weren't officially due for almost three weeks, Fiona's girth had become rather substantial, which in turn had had made her increasingly irritable and clumsy. Not that the boys would dare mention such a thing – they weren't that foolhardy, after all.

Despite their earlier agreement not to find out, Alex and Peter finally gave into their curiosity and discovered that they were going to be blessed with daughters – and what pampered princesses they were going to be.

"They'll be a proper handful come their teenage years," taunted Fiona. "Some of the things me and my friends got up to…"

"And don't you go giving them any ideas," warned Alex, only half-joking.

"I'm sure that with either of our DNA that was going to be the case no matter their gender," taunted Peter.

"Probably." Alex's head began filling with remembrances of all the mischief he got up to as a teen.

May the gods have mercy on us!

Thankfully, his thoughts were soon turned back to the present as the threesome headed homewards to prepare for the baby shower they were hosting that very night. When they reached the complex, Fiona commenced her slow shuffle-waddle ascent back to her apartment to rest up before the big event, while Alex and Peter rushed upstairs to clean their apartment from top to bottom. Once the canapés and cocktails were set up and ready to go, the lads discovered they still had a bit of time before their invitees were due to appear, so they took the opportunity to indulge in a hurried spot of fucking in the shower. Several pleasure-filled minutes later, both their loads had been successfully lightened; their shared good mood lingering as they began to greet their arriving guests.

Amongst the well-wishers was Derek, who had taken some convincing to come due to his guilt over what had happened. Even so, he appeared a tad uneasy when first walking in the door.

"So glad you made it," greeted Peter warmly.

"I'm just happy that you still wanted me here," replied Derek.

"Nonsense! You're family," declared Peter. "What's past is past."

"Yes, it's all fine," reaffirmed Alex.

"Just keep your lips to yourselves," warned Peter, which instantly brought about identical looks of dismay from Alex and Derek. "Just kidding! Honestly, you two are so easy to tease."

Alex swatted Peter on the buttocks in retaliation but was relieved that the unpleasantness seemed to be well behind them now. After exchanging relatively guilt-free smiles, Alex led Derek into the apartment to mix with the other guests, while Peter went off to fetch some more canapés from the kitchen.

Later that evening, the apartment was filled to bursting with their nearest and dearest, and the wonderful array of presents they'd brought with them – there were stuffed animals and baby apparel as far as the eye could see. Indeed, the guys were rather overwhelmed by the support and thoughtfulness of their friends. Some kind souls had even chipped in for a full weekend of spa treatments for Fiona, to help with her recovery after the birth. For her part, Fiona was so overcome with emotion that she very nearly burst into tears, although to be honest anything was likely to set her off these days – it had been a laundry detergent commercial the previous day…damn pregnancy hormones!

After a few hours of merriment, most of the guests had departed, including Fiona who was seen home by a doting Owen. The expectant fathers, along with several of the partygoers, decided to head out for one last hurrah before their parental commitments truly took hold.

Robert had gotten a handful of guest passes to Damnation – one of the perks of their contract – so that the lads could really make a night of it. Only a few of the group had already been, so they were all rather excited at the prospect of the mischief that they could get up to. And so, the happy group, eleven of them in total, got themselves ready, and with the air of excited schoolboys, caught the bus to Limehouse where the club was located.

Upon arriving, they were surprised, and quite pleased, to discover that it was actually the monthly Underwear Party, meaning they had to store their clothes in plastic bags at the coat check. None of the lads were particularly shy, if anything it added to the thrill of the evening.

Given their recent troubles, Alex couldn't help but be a tad hesitant to proceed, as he didn't wish to upset their rediscovered happiness.

"You sure about this?" asked Alex tentatively.

"It'll be fun," replied Peter reassuringly. "It's not like you're going off to an orgy by yourself. Let's just relax and enjoy ourselves before we become buried in dirty diapers and three am feedings."

"OK. If you insist!"

It was a male-only night and the familiar scent of testosterone-fueled action – a delightful mixture of cum, saliva and sweat – soon had all their cocks stirring in anticipation. The crowd ranged both in age and stages of fitness – something for all tastes really. It helped that there were rather eye-opening displays just about everywhere one looked…the place practically screamed depravity. After they'd all stripped off, the guys split up into smaller groups to have a proper wander about the club. Alex and Peter freely let their friends run off without them, as they were content to explore by themselves.

The venue itself was a shadowy, cavernous space with three mezzanines and a huge basement area. On the ground floor, there was a large, brightly-lit stage on the right hand side, used for acts of a more professional nature, whereas a smaller platform facing opposite was set up for use by the more extroverted clientele who were inspired to put on amateur shows. For encouragement, there was a system whereby members of the audience were able to buy drink vouchers and 'tip' the performers for their hard work. Currently, there was a pair of striking redheads engaged in a frenzied bout of fucking, much to the viewing pleasure of the crowd.

To the right of the stages, there was a DJ booth set up on a podium and a largish area for dancing beneath it, which was populated with men grinding and sweating away to the music. In the far left corner at the back of the dance floor, there was a doorway to a small, long room with five slings hanging in a row and ample supplies of gloves and grease set at intervals along a ledge that ran the length of the room – for gentlemen who preferred a more hands-in approach to their pleasure. As Alex passed the entrance, he noticed several gents already hard at work and thought he recognized a few of the fisters and fistees, all putting on quite the spectacle. Apparently, there was quite an art to it, at both ends of the proceedings. Judging by the sounds emanating from the recipients of such handiwork, it seemed as if there were several experienced hands in attendance.

Along the back wall of the main room there was a row of urinals out in the open for the less shy patrons. What Alex didn't realize at first, but soon discovered when he and Peter investigated the basement area, was that a room had been placed directly underneath where gentlemen with a penchant for golden showers could lay down and soak up the warm rain that fell from above. Besides that, there was another doorway, which led to a mini-labyrinth where men could engage in all kinds of wayward behavior in the dark, narrow passages. In fact, Alex caught of glimpse of Sam doing just that with Aaron, the masseur, who had become something of a regular playmate for his perennially promiscuous friend.

The downstairs level also contained an orgy room equipped with numerous black vinyl-covered mattresses – best for cleaning. The lighting was a dim red, adding to the wonderfully seedy atmosphere. The space was already rather full of amorous men going about their business, making the air humid with the heat of their play. Moisture dripped from the ceiling and back down over the writhing forms, as boundaries were pushed and bodies were stretched to their limits. The play looked quite rough – it was the crowd for it after all – and there was much slapping of asses, chests and faces, with a hint of ball torture thrown in for good measure. There was definitely no lovemaking going on, just pure primal lust with men using and abusing one another for their basest needs, violating and raiding each other's welcoming holes. Indeed, the room was filled with a veritable cockcophony of pleasure.

It didn't surprise Alex in the slightest to see that William, Ryan, Matt and Robert were smack bang in the middle of the action, apparently enjoying themselves immensely, and he felt a slight pang of envy. After watching for a few minutes, Alex very much wanted to throw himself into the fray but daren't make such a suggestion to his husband, even though he could see by the look on Peter's face that he too was quite appreciative of the decadent display before them.

I don't want to risk ruining everything.

"Upstairs?" asked Alex, trying to remove himself from the imminent temptation.

"Sure," agreed Peter amiably.

The couple soon found themselves back on the ground floor facing the main stage, where they reunited with Gus and George, who wore matching grins of delight at their surroundings. Set up on the stage there were three functioning wooden stocks, where patrons could be locked in, their hindquarters exposed to the audience, and receive their just punishments. Other patrons were permitted to play with the captives – whipping, spanking, violating with toys and so on – all under the watchful gaze of Master Vic, who made sure that nothing got too out of hand. The

Master in question was an arresting individual, with an imposing muscular build, cropped blond hair, penetrating brown eyes and a sizeable appendage that caused the crotch of his leather pants to bulge promisingly. His whole presence radiated control, an impression further enforced when he issued commands in his deep, gravelly voice.

Only one of the stocks was currently occupied, by a skinny blond twink who had somehow managed to take an extremely large butt plug, which looked as if it would have had to displace his internal organs to fit. It's astounding how adaptable bodies can be in the pursuit of pleasure.

There's no way I could ever fit that…well not without a fair few drinks first!

"Who's next?" demanded Master Vic, his eyes scanning the crowd for eager volunteers.

Peter looked towards Alex and gave him an inquiring look coupled with a cheeky grin. Before Alex had time to respond to Peter's unspoken question, George enthusiastically caught the attention of Master Vic and then proceeded to drag an unquestioningly obedient Gus towards the stage with him. The lads quickly made their way to the small wooden stairs to the left and were soon being welcomed on stage, to the cheers of the raucous crowd. Once they were locked in securely, Master Vic chose a few other lucky lads from the audience to come up and have their wicked way with the trapped men.

Did Petey really want to do that? Wishful thinking. Maybe?

Alex looked on with great amusement as his friends' underwear was ripped down around their ankles leaving them completely vulnerable to the amorous advances of strangers.

They were bitten, licked, spanked, fingered and wanked…and that was all within the first ten minutes.

Situated on the other side of the stocks was a raised dais that Master Vic walked along and randomly shoved his nine thick uncut inches into their helpless mouths – after having released his erection from its leather confinement – as well as occasionally slapping and spitting in their faces.

Damn that looks so hot! They must be having a grand time of it. Lucky sods!

Looking towards his husband, Alex could see a rapt expression on Peter's face and a prominent swelling in his jocks in response to the erotic sight.

"Do you need some help with that?" asked Alex mischievously.

"Yes, I most certainly do, kind Sir."

Looking around to find somewhere with a modicum of privacy, Alex thought he spied the perfect spot. Grabbing Peter's hand, Alex led his husband across the floor, to the circular metal staircase that led up to a small mezzanine above the main bar. It wasn't until they reached the platform that they noticed that a couple of amorous men had already claimed the spot and were engaged in a vigorous bout of play on a sturdy-looking black leather lounge.

A lean, tattooed lad – clad only a pair of shiny, black, knee-high leather boots – was being savagely fucked by a handsome muscle bear…and enjoying it immensely if his grunts and moans were any indication. They stood there enjoying the show for a few moments before Alex realized that he actually knew one of the participants.

I wonder if he's dancing here tonight as well.

"It's Gideon," Alex informed Peter.

"George and Gus' new flat mate?" asked Peter.

"That's the one."

"He certainly takes it like a champ," observed Peter, a touch of admiration in his voice.

Several seconds later, the muscle bear let out a fierce growl...obviously climaxing in the lad beneath him. He pulled out, threw his condom into the nearby bin and slapped his companion on the ass.

"All yours," declared the grinning muscle bear, as he passed the boys and headed back downstairs.

Gideon stayed lying on the couch looking up at Alex and Peter with hungry eyes, his legs still spread invitingly wide. Apparently, recognizing Alex, Gideon gestured for the couple to come closer.

Every fiber of Alex's body screamed for him to jump on top of Gideon but he held himself back. Alex turned towards Peter with every intention of suggesting they find another location to consummate their lust when his husband took him by surprise.

"Wanna take him on?" queried Peter, an impish regard flitting about his features.

"Really?" demanded Alex, slightly incredulous. "But I thought you were happy being monogamous?"

"I am. You know that I love being with only you but I thought it might be fun to have one last spot of naughtiness. I mean it's not cheating if we're doing it together, after all. But if you don't want to play with him and have it only be us, then I'm fine with that as well. It's up to you, Lex."

Conflicted, Alex was unsure which path to pursue. He understood his husband's logic and parts of him were undeniably eager to oblige but he'd already tortured himself a great deal about his less-than-pure thoughts towards other men.

It would so hot to play with him. Will it make things strange between us again? But it's his idea!

"If you're really sure?" asked Alex, seeking final confirmation.

In response, Peter simply took Alex by the hand and led him to the couch where Gideon was still keenly waiting for company. Tearing down their underwear and casting it aside, the lads promptly joined Gideon on the couch and came together in a passionate embrace of tongues and limbs. The couch beneath them was slick with a pungent mixture of spent seed and lube…the muscle bear had been the third guy to bugger Gideon there that evening.

Sandwiching Gideon in the middle, Alex and Peter both ran their hands down his smooth, wet body, scratching and tweaking as they went. Taking a firm grip of Gideon's manhood, Alex proceeded to jack it slowly while he hungrily bit at the dancer's neck. Meanwhile, Peter was massaging and tugging firmly on Gideon's smooth, heavy ball sack, while his mouth focused on attacking the erect dark-pink nipples.

For his part, Gideon was thrashing about like a trapped animal, although he gave no indication of wanting to escape. His frantic movements only increased when Alex and Peter each moved a hand lower, their fingers meeting at the exposed rosebud and then forced their way in together. Their digits worked in tandem, stretching and probing the surprisingly tight hole, rubbing over his prostrate one after the other, causing Gideon to jerk and shake even more violently between them.

After a few more minutes of this delightful torture, Alex removed his digit, stood up and grabbed a condom from the dispenser on the wall and suited himself up. Returning to the couch, Alex roughly flipped Gideon onto his stomach, lined himself up with the welcoming target and slammed into the already well-lubed ass. Taking his cues from his husband, Peter maneuvered around so that he could feed his deliciously fat manhood to a very cock hungry Gideon.

Holding Gideon's hips in a powerful clench locking him in place, Alex pistoned away, slamming inside, their skin loudly smacking together. Alex's nostrils were filled with the intoxicating, heady scent of manly passion, making him even harder as he pounded away.

Looking up from the pleasing sight of his manhood repeatedly disappearing in between the firm buttocks, Alex caught Peter's eye and they moved forward into a passionate embrace. Coming together above Gideon's writhing back, their tongues swirling around one another, as they defiled the man beneath them. Perspiration dripped down both their bodies and onto their playmate, who was already magnificently slick and shiny with god knows how many bodily fluids.

Not wanting to blow quite yet, Alex signaled to Peter and they both pulled out. Alex roughly rolled Gideon onto his back, and very much appreciated the view, especially the way the dancer's Prince Albert piercing glistened in the red light.

Peter promptly suited up and took the place recently vacated by his husband, while Alex moved around to shove his thick inches down Gideon's velvety throat. As they pumped away, both Alex and Peter gripped and grabbed at the slippery, straining body between them. The gogo dancer grunted and whimpered as the couple eagerly used him in their debauched masculine pursuits.

After they had been spit-roasting their willing meat for a good ten minutes, the couple exchanged an understanding look and pulled out. The pair stood over Gideon, cocks at the ready, determined to spread their semen all over his smooth skin. The highly charged situation had them both near the edge of release and the rapid hand movements that followed soon brought about the desired result, leaving Gideon covered head–to-toe in fresh, warm cream. Alex's load had spurted over Gideon's face and dripped down his chest while Peter's coated his stomach, crotch and legs.

When they were both fully spent, Alex and Peter grabbed an arm each and pulled Gideon up into a seated position, in order to repay all his hard work. They proceeded to work his body over – tweaking his nipples, tugging at his heavy, pendulous balls and generally molesting him – while he jacked himself off. The excessive stimulation his body had taken over the past hour took its toll and a mere thirty seconds later he added his own contribution to the creamy concoction, streaking its way down his lithe form. The threesome then came back together, kissing and stroking one another, as the mixture of their combined loads spread between them. Some minutes later, Gideon broke away with an air of reluctance.

"Thanks lads, you were awesome but I gotta go clean up before my next show."

And with that he retrieved his crumpled blue and black jockstrap from beside the couch and traipsed off downstairs to wash himself at one of the showers next to the restrooms – they were often used by patrons and staff alike to rinse away the remnants of their play.

Electing to stay exactly where they were, Alex and Peter continued to hold one another and gently kiss, as the party kept in full swing below them. They rested there for quite some time just enjoying the feel of one another's sticky nakedness. Lying in Peter's arms, Alex felt snug and secure, and very happy with his world, indeed.

I could stay right here forever…

Eventually, the couple decided to try and find their friends and, with great effort, roused themselves to head back downstairs. As they were passing the smaller stage, Alex's eye was caught by familiar figures. Upon the platform were the throuple – Dean, Mac and Tom – who appeared to be coming to the end of a rather inspiring performance, given the overflowing tip jar and the throng that had gathered to watch. The show went on for another five minutes or so, and Alex couldn't pull himself away – neither could Peter for that matter. It thrilled him to see his best friend enjoying himself in such a delightful manner and, honestly, it was a scene he had imagined once or twice during a hearty round of self-pleasuring. Predictably, their show ended with the threesome dripping with each other's sticky seed and complementary looks of satisfaction upon their handsome faces.

"Good job," complimented Alex, when the throuple had climbed down from the stage.

"You boys certainly know how to put on a great show," added Peter with a wink.

"Thanks, we aim to please," said Dean, before collecting their hard-earned tips and heading off to the showers with his boyfriends.

Turing towards the main stage, Alex and Peter soon found the others in their party who had managed to regroup after their various sexploits. It was time for the finale of the evening with Master Vic presenting a special show involving the poor tortured twink from before, who hadn't yet been released – although he still appeared to be a rather willing participant. The blond looked familiar to Alex but he couldn't quite put his finger on where he knew him from. It wasn't until he accidentally caught a knowing look passing between William and Ryan that Alex made the connection.

Their apartment! It's Hunter! He's certainly a welcoming lad.

Gideon was now also on stage, still wearing his boots but his jockstrap had been replaced by a leather harness that ran across his chest, then downwards to wrap around his manhood and back up to his neck where it connected to a leash, onto which Master Vic kept a tight hold. Having fully recuperated from his time amusing the patrons, Gideon was faithfully doing his Master's bidding – which mostly seemed to revolve around seeing how much punishment Hunter could take before begging for mercy.

Master Vic was using all sorts of props in his efforts – even an orange traffic cone at one point – much to the great delight of the onlookers...Alex and his friends most definitely included. Truthfully, more than a few of those watching would have gleefully traded places with the young, blond captive in a heartbeat.

Quite a lot of minutes later, Master Vic apparently decided that the tasty twink had undeniably proved his manhood. In all likelihood, he could have molested Hunter all night long without even a squeak of protest – judging by the wicked glint in his eye that's certainly what he had planned for him after the performance was finished.

Finally, it was time for the grand finale, which involved Master Vic releasing his playthings from their servitude. Then he positioned them at either side of the front edge of the stage before placing himself in the center between them. The tempting trio then jerked their erections while facing the crowd. Their natural release came all too quickly and they were soon showering the adoring audience with a refreshing white spray. Hunter, whose load had been building for about five hours even managed to hit guys over six feet away.

"Fucking hell!" exclaimed Peter.

"You took the words right out of my mouth," agreed Alex.

"I've got something else to put back in there if you like," countered Peter, grabbing a hold of Alex's left hand and placing it on his member that was stretching the underwear in its excitement.

"Lead the way!"

Hand in hand, the couple wandered downstairs to lose themselves in a dark corner and fulfill their husbandly duties to another once more. All in all, it was truly a night to remember.

* * *

In the very early hours of the last Monday in October, just over a week past the due date, Alex received a call from Fiona who had awakened to a thoroughly wet bed.

"It's time!" squealed Fiona breathlessly.

"You're sure?" demanded Alex groggily.

"It's either that or someone switched in a waterbed while I was asleep." It was hard to miss the certain touch of irritability to her voice. "So, get your butts over here...NOW!"

"OK, OK. We'll be right over."

After hastily waking up his heavily slumbering husband, Alex and Peter were dressed and out the door in a matter of minutes. Both of them had had their phones practically glued to their hands for the past few weeks just in case, but it seemed like the girls were content to take their time and be fashionably late.

Proof that they're already fabulous.

In an effort to hasten their arrival, Fiona had tried several of the remedies suggested to her on the pregnancy forum – eating spicy food and bananas, primrose oil, acupuncture and even a spot of nipple stimulation – but all to no avail. Dr. Gillian Parker had even brought up the option of inducing Fiona if she hadn't gone into labor by the following Wednesday.

The expectant dads-to-be rushed over to the neighboring building and helped a surprisingly calm Fiona downstairs to their car and drove as fast as safety allowed to St. Luke's Hospital. In comparison to Fiona's relatively relaxed demeanor, the guys were nervous wrecks and practically beside themselves with a bubbling mixture of anxious excitement and glee.

I can't believe that they're nearly here!

Over the previous weeks, Alex and Peter had driven to the hospital several times, wanting to make sure they had the route down pat and were able to get there as quickly as possible. In the end, their practice had been for naught, as given the early hour the traffic was pretty much non-existent, allowing the trio to arrive a mere ten minutes later. Once she'd been admitted, Fiona was settled into her private birthing suite and clearly eager to get the babies out as soon as possible. Due to the earliness of the day, the guys decided not to call anyone else, as they didn't want to disturb everyone's sleep, although the prospective grandparents undoubtedly wouldn't have minded at all.

When Gillian arrived, around thirty minutes later, Fiona's contractions were still too far apart for the delivery to begin in earnest. A few hours passed and the trio was beginning to wonder if the girls were ever going to leave their comfy cocoon.

"I'm going to be pregnant forever!" wailed Fiona.

A few more nervous hours passed, where the guys did their very best to keep Fiona as comfortable and supported as possible.

"Would you like some more ice?" asked Alex.

"Do you need another pillow," inquired Peter.

"How about one of you pushes these damn things out for me instead!" cried Fiona, in an increasingly frustrated state.

"Would like something more for the pain?" Dr. Parker offered in her habitually serene manner.

"Dear gods, YES!" insisted Fiona. "I'll take everything you've got!"

After her epidural, Fiona was in a measurably better mood – much to their collective relief. Not that the guys or medical staff had been particularly surprised or offended by her increasingly irate and curse-filled mutterings as the labor wore on.

A little over an hour later, it was time, and after quite a few momentous pushes the babies emerged, one right after the other, with no complications and fairly healthy sets of lungs, judging by their cries upon being introduced to the big, bright world. After they'd been checked over and cleaned up a little, Fiona was first to hold the newborns …only fair considering all the effort she'd put into bringing them into the world. A few minutes later, a happily tearful Fiona handed them over to the proud papas.

"Here are your beautiful daughters!"

"They're perfect," exclaimed Alex, his face full of pure love.

"That they are," agreed Peter, sharing the same visage.

"Hello, Emily." Alex greeted their first born, his eyes gleaming with happiness.

"Hi, Sarah," welcomed Peter, to the bundle nestled in his arms.

During the long wait, the guys had messaged their nearest and dearest about the impending birth. So by the time they'd made their grand entrance, the waiting room was packed with their families and closest friends. Once the babies were installed in the hospital nursery, the lads showed them off to a steady stream of visitors who were all clamoring for a peek at the new arrivals.

Two days later, when they were properly settled back in at home with their daughters, Alex and Peter officially announced the twins' arrival to the rest of the world via social media – the joys of modern living. This in turn had prompted many a heartfelt congratulation from friends and acquaintances from all around the globe, which warmed their hearts greatly.

I can't believe I'm a dad!

* * *

Six months later, Alex was enjoying the gentle warmth of the late summer's day, as he pushed the twins around their flower-filled local park in their navy-blue double stroller. It was a daily ritual they performed – weather permitting – that had the dual benefit of letting Alex leave the apartment and lulling his daughters into a peaceful slumber. Unfortunately, these days, it was close to the only exercise Alex got and his frame had become much more bearier in build. Not that he was too troubled, as he was still caught up in the joy of being a new father.

Many sleepless nights had followed the birth, of course; particularly so during the first four months, as one baby always seemed to be waking up the other. That being said, as tired as they both were, Alex and Peter were the happiest they had ever been. Fortunately, they'd had no shortage of willing babysitters to help ease their sleep deprivation on occasion – Fiona and Owen among the most regular volunteers. Help even came from those they hadn't thought would be keen, like Sam, who displayed a thoroughly paternal streak in his fondness for the babies.

Admittedly, it had been a hard on Alex when Peter had very reluctantly gone back to work about a month after the birth. To his great amazement, Alex hadn't been as completely overwhelmed as he'd feared when he'd begun to shoulder the majority of the daily childrearing. It had, however, taken at least four cups of bitterly strong coffee per day, to keep him relatively functional and avoid simply devolving into a nappy-changing, bottle-feeding zombie.

As much as Alex and Peter loved their little bundles of joy, words cannot describe the relief they felt when the twins had both finally started to sleep through the night about a month earlier. Not that they were eager for them to grow up too fast mind you, which would bring its own new set of worries.

I hope they aren't as boy-crazy as I was.

Whenever all four of them went out together as a family, they often drew attention. Indeed, people often openly remarked to them what a picture-perfect family they made, which pleased Alex and his husband no end.

It also hadn't escaped Alex's notice that when he ventured out solo with the twins, he often drew looks of interest from men and women alike – apparently babies make the perfect wing women.

Looks like I'm finally a DILF!

After completing their habitual ten laps, Alex approached the far left gate of the park, which was opened and held by a polite young gent, with a mess of auburn curls and a friendly smile, on his way in with a picnic basket.

"Thanks, so much" said Alex, while maneuvering the stroller through the less-than-accommodating gate.

"No problem…they are so adorable," enthused the man, catching a glimpse of the dozing infants.

"For the moment, anyway," joked Alex. "Have a lovely day."

As he wearily pushed the stroller through the gate, and out towards home, Alex looked down at his sweetly, slumbering daughters and smiled to himself.

This is the life.

ABOUT THE AUTHOR

Jimi could be considered to be something of a refined blend of Australian/Polish heritage – given his passion for the arts, vodka and BBQs. He now lives in Paris with his wonderfully understanding French husband and cats.

For other of his raunchy ramblings and published work, feel free to browse http://www.jimify.me follow him on Twitter & Instagram @jimifyme or show your devotion at facebook.com/JIMIFY.ME

DIGITAL TITLES BY JIMI GONINAN

DOM'S DELIGHTS 1:

DOM'S DELIGHTS 2: BACHELOR PARTY BLOWOUT

DOM'S DELIGHTS 3: HUSBANDLY DUTIES

MILE HIGH CUB

LOVE THE SINNER

UNDERWEAR MAKETH THE MAN

BEST SERVED HOT

LUST AFTER DEATH

ON THE NAUGHTY LIST

AIN'T NO SAINT

A MAN FOR EVERY OCCASION

THE VIRGIN HEART

For all Jimi's titles please visit his page at lydianpress.com

IN PRINT FROM LYDIAN PRESS

DOM'S DELIGHTS

Come on in and taste the love!

Dom has worked hard pursuing his dreams of delighting the masses with his tasty treats - indeed his cream has been eagerly eaten all about the town. Now he has almost everything he ever dreamed of – a successful business, loving friends and a beautiful beau. There's just one more thing he needs to make his life complete...to finally marry the man of his dreams!

BEST SERVED HOT

Revenge has never been sweeter.

When Jameson loses everything he holds dear, he almost drowns in a sea of despair. Bitter and broken, he shuns his friends and retreats from the world. Then a chance encounter with a handsome young man offers him a glimmer of hope, and he slowly begins to piece his life back together. Will he be given the second chance at the love he so desperately deserves?

A MAN FOR EVERY OCCASION

There's always time for love.

The bustling city of Port Davinica is home to many stories of love, lust and more than a few happy endings. Follow the adventures of these men as they find love in all manner of places with an amorous touch of the supernatural thrown in for good measure. You'll soon discover in this collection of romantic tales that no matter the festive occasion – Halloween, Christmas, and especially Valentine's Day - there's always time for love.

THE VIRGIN HEART

Some things are worth waiting for.

Abraham Chadwick is locked in a state of quiet desperation. Not only has he never been kissed, he's never even been in love. Indeed, as Abraham prepares for college, he's beginning to fret that he may stay a virgin forever. Fortunately, the sudden arrival of a handsome Southern gentleman into his world gives him a new sense of hope. Will Abraham finally find the love and affection that he's so desired for so long?

Lydian Press is dedicated to bringing you the finest
GLBTQ erotic literature on the web.

Visit us on the web at:

http://lydianpress.com

www.ingramcontent.com/pod-product-compliance
Lightning Source LLC
Chambersburg PA
CBHW061159170626
46809CB00003B/1174